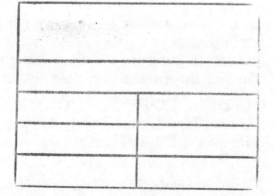

SPECIAL MESSAGE TO READERS

THE ULVERSCROFT FOUNDATION
(registered UK charity number 264873)
was established in 1972 to provide funds for
research, diagnosis and treatment of eye diseases.
Examples of major projects funded by
the Ulverscroft Foundation are:-

- The Children's Eye Unit at Moorfields Eye Hospital, London
- The Ulverscroft Children's Eye Unit at Great Ormond Street Hospital for Sick Children
- Funding research into eye diseases and treatment at the Department of Ophthalmology, University of Leicester
- The Ulverscroft Vision Research Group, Institute of Child Health
- Twin operating theatres at the Western Ophthalmic Hospital, London
- The Chair of Ophthalmology at the Royal Australian College of Ophthalmologists

You can help further the work of the Foundation
by making a donation or leaving a legacy.
Every contribution is gratefully received. If you
would like to help support the Foundation or
require further information, please contact:

THE ULVERSCROFT FOUNDATION
The Green, Bradgate Road, Anstey
Leicester LE7 7FU, England
Tel: (0116) 236 4325

website: www.foundation.ulverscroft.com

A QUESTION OF LOVE

As a partner in Kershaw & Co., Roseanne has very clear plans for her career and her life. She is fiercely independent, and has no time for anything outside of work — until she meets Euan Kennedy, the nephew of her business partner, Mr Kershaw. Euan is funny, warm, charming — and drop-dead gorgeous. But when Euan doubts Roseanne's integrity, the feelings that have started to grow between them are dashed. How can she ever love a man who thinks so little of her?

GWEN KIRKWOOD

A QUESTION OF LOVE

Complete and Unabridged

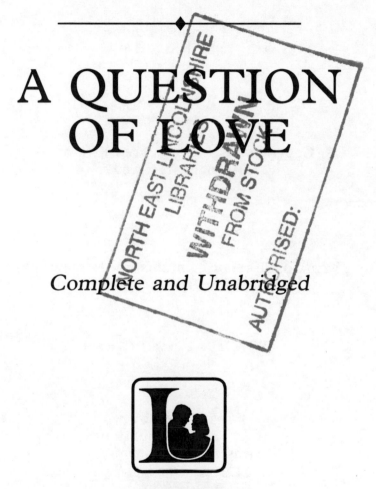

LINFORD
Leicester

First published in Great Britain in 2013

First Linford Edition
published 2016

A catalogue record for this book is available
from the British Library.

ISBN 978–1–4448–2765–1

Published by
F. A. Thorpe (Publishing)
Anstey, Leicestershire

Set by Words & Graphics Ltd.
Anstey, Leicestershire
Printed and bound in Great Britain by
T. J. International Ltd., Padstow, Cornwall

This book is printed on acid-free paper

1

'Never underestimate an intelligent woman who is in a position of authority,' Euan Kennedy recalled his mother's advice, 'especially if she has the respect of her colleagues. Such a woman has to be twice as worthy as a man to have achieved her position. She will not be the sort of bimbo who succumbs to your charming smile, my boy. It might not be good for your ego but it would teach you a lesson. Indeed,' she had added, with a gleam in her eye, which might have been described as malevolent had she not been his ever-loving mother, 'I hope you do meet such a woman one day.'

Did he need a lesson? Had success gone to his head? Surely not. Yet he couldn't deny he was irked by Rose-anne Fairfax, and he was beginning to wonder whether she was the type his mother had had in mind. Certainly all the staff seemed to like and respect her. But . . .

'Whew!' Euan whistled in surprise as his gaze travelled over the computer screen at end of his first week at Kershaw & Company. 'So Uncle Simon's P.A. is not entirely the Miss Perfect he believes,' he muttered to himself, 'in spite of the aloof, touch-me-not persona she presents.' He had a strong suspicion Miss Fairfax did not trust him with the firm's computer systems, but on what grounds he had no idea. Especially considering he had built up a successful IT business of his own from scratch. His eyes returned to the computer screen and he stifled a spontaneous bark of laughter, but a chuckle still rumbled deep in his chest when he glanced through the glass partition at Roseanne Fairfax in the adjoining office. He appreciated the dry wit evident in her email. Maybe time spent at his uncle's business premises would not be so dull after all. He never could resist a challenge and Miss Fairfax's icy demeanour had already proved resistant to his usual brand of charm, not to mention the fact that she refuted his right to take over his uncle's office.

It had not taken him long to realise she was popular with all the staff, from the factory foreman to the administration staff in the office. He had noted the beaming smile she gave the middle-aged door keeper when she arrived in the mornings. They all spoke of her with warmth and respect and he would have had to be blind not to notice she was damned attractive.

'Not everything is as it seems though,' he murmured to himself as he re-read the email she had written. Uncle Simon's Miss Perfect was not without a bit of humour, he admitted, even if it was at his expense — at least this time. His mouth firmed as he resolved to get his own back. Euan knew, without conceit, that he was reasonably good-looking. He was intelligent and he had worked hard and used his abilities, as the success of his business had proved. Above all, he was not used to being ignored — especially by women. He was both irked and intrigued by the indifference Miss Fairfax had displayed towards him since he arrived.

He had volunteered to install the new computer system in the offices of his uncle's meat processing plant during Simon Kershaw's absence, but he usually left the checking and tweaking to one of his subordinates. This job had been a spur-of-the-moment assignment to occupy him while he was here though, so there was nothing for it but to attend to any final adjustments to the program himself. He always knew exactly what was required whenever he undertook a new program, but on this occasion he didn't exactly have a free rein. For the first time in his life he was not sure why he had changed his plans at the last minute.

He had made careful arrangements so that he could be away from his

US-based company while he visited his mother in Australia. It had been a shock to him when he learned she had undergone a major operation without telling him, and while he was relieved to hear she was making an excellent recovery, he wanted to make sure she was well looked after. Apparently the news had also been a shock to Uncle Simon, because he too had made plans to visit his only sister while she was recuperating. There was no doubt her brother's proposed visit had been a pleasant surprise which his mother was eagerly anticipating. There seemed no point in both of them visiting at the same time, so Euan had decided to break his journey to Australia and visit Scotland instead, allowing his uncle and mother time alone together to catch up.

So here he was at Kershaw & Company, his Uncle Simon's meat processing plant in Scotland, while the boss himself was on the other side of the world. Euan's eyes gleamed with devilish amusement as he re-read the email which had never been intended for his eyes.

*   *   *

In her own office Roseanne muttered in irritation and wondered why she felt so restless. Why was she so aware of the man across the passage? She had been left in sole charge of Kershaw & Co. scores of times while Mr K went off on his meat buying trips. Why should it be any different this time? And why should she be so on edge? During her holidays from university she had wanted to earn some money, so at various times she had worked in almost every part of the factory. She had got to know the staff and the different systems. She understood the routines, how the processing and packaging plants operated, and why certain things had to be done to comply with health and safety and hygiene regulations. The experience had proved invaluable, even though her mother had irritably declared at the time that it bore no relation to her degree in accountancy.

She had known Simon Kershaw since she was a child. He had been like an adopted uncle when she was young. They got on well together. When she finished at university he had confessed that keeping records and accounts was not his strong suite, especially now the company was beginning to expand, so he had offered her a permanent position in charge of the office staff and the accounts at Kershaw & Co. She had accepted. On several occasions she had proved herself more than capable of dealing with problems and she could handle the administration of the business blindfolded — well almost. Perhaps it would be better if she was blindfolded; then she wouldn't be so conscious of Mr K's nephew now occupying the boss's office right next to hers; she wouldn't see his long legs taking the stairs two at a time to Mr K's spacious flat above the offices either.

What right did Euan Kennedy have to come here out of the blue and assume so much authority? She felt he was taking over her space, as well as his uncle's. She had an uneasy premonition he might take her over completely if she was not careful.

No! She thumped the desk. She didn't allow anyone to interfere with her work, though plenty had tried. The trouble was, Mr K had never travelled half way round the world before, nor been away for as long as three whole months. He had been terribly upset when he heard about his sister's operation. Although they kept in touch regularly, it was years since they had seen each other; her illness had filled him with consternation and jolted him into action, hence the trip to Australia.

'You see, lassie,' he had explained, 'Aileen is all the family I have. She's had a serious operation and it's made me realise neither of us will be here forever and I ought to go and see her.' He had given Roseanne his boyish smile. 'I might even give some of your ideas a try if I see their electronic machines in action over there.'

'I'll believe that when I see it!' She had grinned at him. They both knew he hated change, and he avoided anything to do with computers if he could. She hadn't dared suggest any changes down at Ashburn — the organic farm they owned between them, thanks to Grandfather Fairfax. One step at a time was her motto when leading Mr K into the modern world of technology.

'Aileen has a son,' he had said, 'but I havenae seen him since he was a wee laddie. He's built up a business developing computerised machinery. He travels all over the world. I'll give him a ring and let him know I'm going to visit his mother. If I meet him there I might invite him to come over to Scotland for a visit. He could give us his advice on modernising some of the processing plant when I return. It's time I got to know the boy.'

Euan Kennedy had responded to his

call quicker than either of them could have anticipated. He explained his sudden decision to break his journey and visit Scotland, the land of his birth, now he knew his Uncle Simon was already booked to travel to Australia himself. Uncle and nephew had met briefly at the airport. Roseanne knew all about the plans, but now Euan Kennedy was sitting in Mr K's office as though he owned the place, and he had made it plain he planned to stay until his uncle returned. So far he had been too busy installing and checking a new computer system in the offices to interfere with Roseanne's work overseeing the factory, but she had noticed the way he cast his eye over them all whenever he passed by the glass-fronted offices. Annoyingly, his speculative gaze always seemed to linger longest on her. He had one of those assessing sorts of stares, as though his eyes could see inside your head, Roseanne thought irritably. She had never been easily

influenced by the opinions, or attentions, of male colleagues, however
charming they might be, and she made
it a rule never to mix business and
pleasure.

'Oh, drat Euan Kennedy!' she mumbled
aloud, glad she had an office to herself.
That was when she had acted on impulse
and dashed off an email to her sister to
relieve her feelings. Rob would understand her frustration.

★　★　★

Euan contemplated his uncle's parting
words at the airport. 'Whatever you do,
laddie, don't upset Miss Fairfax. I
couldn't run the business without
Roseanne. Together we're a good team
— the best in fact. We complement
each other. We've almost doubled the
business since she joined the company.'

There hadn't been much time for
chat but Euan could still hear his
Uncle's urgent admonition, making
sure he knew how essential his P.A. was

to him and to the company. It had surprised him. His mother had always maintained her brother was a confirmed bachelor who liked to do things his own way.

'I believe you're like him in many ways, Euan,' she'd told him more than once. 'You're both successful in business, but you're thirty now and you still have no serious girlfriends as far I know.' He'd heard the wistful note and the faint question in her voice. He knew she longed to see him settle down and provide her with a brood of grandchildren.

Euan's mental picture of his uncle's P.A. as a middle-aged woman dressed in a smart grey jacket and skirt, with a hatchet face and grey hair worn in a bun, couldn't have been more wrong. He guessed Roseanne Fairfax was at least five years younger than him; she was tall and slim, with the fair skin which went with her auburn hair — well, not auburn exactly because it shone like a golden halo when the sun came through her office window in the afternoons. If he ever got close enough, he could wager there would be a smattering of freckles across the bridge of her small, straight nose. Although her face was an almost perfect oval there was a determined tilt to her chin; her mouth curved upwards at the corners as though ready to smile — except when she stared back at him. Then it straightened, and her green eyes seemed to shoot sparks at him, even before he began asking her questions about the way his uncle's business was run. Her thick hair was coiled in a neat plait around her head. He wondered what it would be like when she let it down to blow free in the wind. If Uncle Simon had ever read his P.A.'s personal emails he might have changed his opinion about some aspects of Roseanne Fairfax's character, he mused.

His grey eyes glinted as he pressed the print button. He would keep a copy of this particular email and enjoy a bit of sport with Miss Fairfax. He watched as the printer sent out a sheet of paper, headed: Kershaw & Co. — Suppliers and Processors of Fine Quality British Meat Products.

Hi Rob — I'm writing this from work because I shall be busy packing this weekend ready for the move to our new flat. My own computer will be off until I get moved and sorted out again. Four weeks before you get back you said? I wish you were here now.

Euan frowned. His mother had been at pains to warn him about Uncle Simon's strict moral standards. What would he say if he discovered his prim and proper Miss Fairfax was moving in with her boyfriend while he was away? He read on.

You'll never believe it, Rob. We're moving into the modern world at last. We've even got broadband,

AND a completely new computer system. It came with a hunk of prime meat too! No, not another of Mr K's prize bullocks. This hunk is Mr K's nephew. He's come over from America, and his name is Euan Kennedy. Mr K. phoned from the airport to warn me of his arrival. He hadn't expected Euan to come to visit until he returned to Scotland himself. He — the nephew — has been closeted in Mr K's office every day so far. I can't help wondering what he is delving into. Gladys and some of the girls keep casting hungry glances whenever he does come out so maybe he's afraid of being processed too! I'm too busy to pay much attention to him, but first impressions are that he's a fair-looking beast with a fine rump on him! I'd say he's been around a bit. Perhaps it's time we played our old tricks again and had a bit of fun?

Must dash now. Miss you lots.

Love Ros. XX

* * *

Called into Mr K's office, Roseanne stared at Euan Kennedy as he sat behind his uncle's desk, regarding her with a smug expression on his handsome face. She was proud of her reputation for efficiency and integrity, and that of her staff too. He cleared his throat, drawing her eyes back to his face. He was eyeing her like a cat with a mouse before it pounced. What was he waiting for? Why was he looking at her so expectantly? She was not used to feeling at a disadvantage. She frowned. She had learned to control the temper that went with her auburn hair but she knew she was in danger of losing it with this infuriating man. Mr K admired her calmness in a crisis. It was one of the reasons he was happy to leave her in charge when he went on his buying trips.

'Cat got your tongue, Miss Fairfax?'

'Not that I'm aware of, Mr Kennedy,' Roseanne retorted. She was tempted to

16

stick it out at him but she knew that would be childish, plus it would undermine the image of efficient and dignified P.A. that she was determined to present to him. 'Is there anything else you want to know?'

'It appears a consignment of prime meat has not been entered in the delivery records.' His expression was bland.

'A consignment not recorded? Are you sure? Mary is meticulous in keeping a record of all deliveries.'

'Maybe she is.' His mouth twitched and Roseanne stared at it, noticing the firm, well-shaped lips and the white, even teeth as he favoured her with a wolfish smile. 'Nevertheless, an acquisition of prime meat was mentioned — or was it fine rump?' The twitching at the corners of his mouth increased and Roseanne's eyes suddenly widened in dismay as realisation dawned.

'Oh no!' she gasped as she recalled her facetious description of him in her email to her sister. Somehow he had managed to read it. It was an unwritten law amongst the office staff that there should be no private emails or use of mobile phones during work. Ever since she had become a permanent part of Kershaw & Co. she had set an example and the girls respected her for it. Now Euan Kennedy, of all people, had caught her out.

'My email to Rob was personal,' she said indignantly, but colour burned in her cheeks. She couldn't deny she had used her work computer for a personal email to Robinia. She tried to recall exactly what she had said. There was only ten months between them in age so they had always been close. As children they even had a language of their own — slang, bordering on rude, their mother called it, a disgrace to the beautiful flowery names she had bestowed upon them. It was true not everyone appreciated their humour, or forgave some of their more outrageous pranks. They were alike in appearance but their interests were almost entirely opposite, except perhaps for books and music.

Robinia was a born flirt, with her dancing eyes and infectious smile. Sometimes Roseanne wished she could be more like that herself but as the elder sister she had always been more serious, absorbing knowledge like a sponge, enjoying a challenge. She prided herself on her organisation and self-control. That was the reason Rob had trusted her to buy the flat and arrange the move — although how long Robinia would stay in one place after so much globe-trotting in her job as a model was debateable. But Roseanne was not too concerned about that. She liked to have her own space. It was one of the reasons she spent most weekends down at the farm near the Scottish Border. She had always felt she could be a free spirit at Ashburn.

She blinked, aware that Euan Kennedy was watching the emotions chasing each other across her expressive face.

'Nobody could read other people's emails before,' she protested. 'Even if he could have read them, Mr Kershaw would never have done so. I doubt if he'd be concerned about this one anyway.'

'No? Obviously he is almost a stranger to me — we've not met since I was five years old, after all — but from what I've heard of his strict morals I don't believe he would approve of you moving in with your boyfriend the minute he's out of the country for three months.' Even to himself Euan knew he sounded like a lecturing old woman, and that was not a part of the email he had intended quoting.

'Boyfr . . . ?' Roseanne almost choked and her eyes widened. She lowered her lashes but not before Euan glimpsed the gold flecks dancing in their green depths. Was she laughing at him? He eyed her keenly, suspicious of her suddenly demure expression. Was she biting her full lower lip to prevent a smile? he wondered indignantly.

Roseanne hoped he couldn't read her mind. When Rob returned they would certainly play a few tricks and enjoy shaking his air of superiority. They had often swapped identities when they were younger. Rob was an expert at winding men around her little finger, only to leave them confused when their next encounter was with Roseanne, so much more cool and reserved.

'The email was on your work computer,' Euan reminded her. 'I understood from Uncle Simon that you were perfection personified, Miss Fairfax. Perhaps it's a case of when the cat's away?'

'No it is not!' she retorted angrily.

'Tut-tut. 'Miss Fairfax is always calm in a crisis, she never loses control,' or so Uncle Simon informed me. 'She never panics or forgets an instruction.' I guessed Uncle Simon's description was too good to be true.' He rose to his feet and came round the desk. She was five feet seven but he was taller. He looked down at her. Roseanne was tempted to swipe the smile from his face. Her green eyes sparked with temper. Euan Kennedy nodded with satisfaction. Miss Efficiency did have hidden depths — how could she not with that abundant flame-coloured hair, even if it was plaited in an elegant coil on top of her neat little head. He imagined seeing it in wild disarray and discovering the passion behind that cool façade. Pity he only had four weeks before the return of Rob, the worthy boyfriend. He went into action.

'Uncle Simon said you would fill me in on everything, including telling me about the farm and the rare breeds of animals he keeps. We'll go down to Ashburn tomorrow morning. We'll have lunch on the way. Don't forget to bring your wellingtons and a change of clothes.'

'I can't do that! Besides . . . ' Her voice trailed away. She did spend almost every weekend at the farm, except when Robinia paid her fleeting visits to Scotland. Although she enjoyed her job and the challenges that Kershaw & Co. presented, she was a country girl at heart.

'Besides?' Euan Kennedy prompted, his grey eyes scrutinising her face. What a determined chin she had — and what a kissable mouth.

'I do spend weekends down there,' admitted Roseanne, 'but I told Mrs Lennox, the housekeeper, I wouldn't be down for the next two weeks, so she has gone to visit her sister in Wales. She has taken the opportunity while Mr Kershaw is away.'

'But you have a key?'

'Yes,' she flushed, 'but . . . '

'But nothing.'

'It's Friday tomorrow,' she snapped.

'So?'

'It is one of the busiest days of the month.'

'This place can tick over while you play hooky.'

'I never play hooky!' Roseanne straightened her slim shoulders even more.

'Okay, so one day without you here will be fine.'

She opened her mouth to protest but Euan Kennedy was used to being in command.

'That's an order.' He watched her eyes narrow and heard her indrawn breath. The tension between them was almost tangible. 'Look,' he said pacifically, 'while my uncle is away I am in charge. If anything goes wrong I shall take full responsibility.' He had intended to sound reassuring but Roseanne's eyes glittered like green emeralds, and just as hard. She had always been in charge any time Simon Kershaw had been away and he had never even hinted that things would be any different this time. He hadn't even known his long-lost nephew would be coming to Scotland until he himself was ready to leave.

'When did you decide to come to Scotland, Mr Kennedy?'

'I decided to stop off here when my uncle informed me he was planning to visit my mother in Australia. I am grateful to him for taking so much time with her when she has been ill. I hope to repay him a little by keeping a close eye on the running of his company during his absence. Also he mentioned modernising some of the processing plant. This will be a splendid opportunity to make an assessment.'

'But you didn't have time to discuss any details at the airport?'

'No . . . ' Euan frowned as he met her steady green gaze. Her measured tones reminded him of being called before the headmaster at school. 'I can't see any reason why I should explain myself to you Miss Fairfax, but during the brief time we spent together at the airport my uncle did ask me to humour you.'

Humour me! Roseanne was furious. *He talks as though I'm a spoiled brat,* she thought to herself. She knew Simon Kershaw would not have used such a demeaning phrase.

'I gathered your meeting had lasted

about forty minutes when your Uncle telephoned to warn me of your arrival,' she said in a steely tone. 'So I'm presuming he had no time to explain to you the way we run things here? Or the various arrangements?'

'He knows I am used to running my own business.'

'A business which is very different from a meat processing factory, yet you have assumed authority without knowing the first thing about our policies here.' Inwardly Roseanne was seething at Euan Kennedy's arrogance, but she wished she was not so aware of his male attractions. Such things had never affected her before. She would have been relieved to know that, to Euan Kennedy, she looked as cool as an ice maiden.

'Since I am family to Simon, I consider it my duty to take charge and look after his interests, especially considering my mother is the reason for his absence.'

'And you think you can do that

knowing nothing about the business?' Roseanne asked with a deceptive sweetness which would have sent warning signals to anyone who knew her. Euan Kennedy saw only a very attractive woman and he had never had any difficulty winning over women before. He gave her one of his charming smiles.

'I'm sure the processing of meat products is pretty basic. I have installed machines far more complicated than Kershaw's is likely to need. We had a brief discussion about more automation.' *Oh yes,* thought Roseanne, *and I've had several discussions, without success.* But the man in front of her was going on smoothly, 'I believe I have persuaded him that most of the processing can be done by computerised robotic machines.'

'Computers are your line of work I believe?'

'Yes, they are,' he said with a slight smile. He had fallen into the world of technology by accident rather than by choice but he had been lucky and his company was worth a considerable sum now. He had not intended to sound patronising but Roseanne interpreted his smile as smug and her temper flared.

'In that case, Mr Kennedy, you stick to your business with computers and I shall stick to mine — taking charge of Kershaw and Co.'

'You can't do that, Miss Fairfax!'

'You think not? I am always in charge in Mr Kershaw's absence. I shall remain so until I hear from him directly telling me he has passed all responsibility for the firm over to you. And if that happens, you can be sure I shall be moving to pastures new immediately.' *And taking my forty-five per cent share in the company with me,* she vowed silently as she turned and left his office.

'Well!' Euan flopped into his chair and pushed his fingers through his thick brown hair. 'Don't upset her,' his uncle had ordered. 'Whatever you do, don't get on the wrong side of Roseanne.'

And at their first real encounter they had crossed enough swords to make sparks fly. He had never had a problem getting his own way with people, even when he was a boy. His mother had always said he had inherited his father's dancing blue-grey eyes and beguiling smile, although she was not without a certain innocent charm herself when it came to getting her way. The aloof Miss Fairfax certainly presented a challenge though, and he was fairly sure she had the passion and the temper to go with her vibrant hair. He loved the colour of it, and the thick tresses which crowned her head like a halo. He longed to draw his fingers through it and feel its silken length.

His mother had always told him he would meet his match one day . . .

2

Roseanne had summoned all her self-control during her confrontation with Euan Kennedy but her legs felt weak by the time she reached her own desk and she sighed with relief when she saw him pick up his car keys, check his personal mobile, then stride out of the office. She watched through the window and saw him driving away in the red sports car which he had ordered to be delivered to the airport in readiness for his arrival. It must be nice to have such confidence and the money to go with it, she thought. She needed time to regain her composure before she saw him again, especially if they were to have another dispute. She had no doubt there would be another, maybe several, before Mr Kershaw returned. Her mouth firmed. She had no intention of allowing Euan Kennedy to browbeat her, but it would have been easier to deal with if he had been older and less attractive.

★　★　★

Euan glanced at his wristwatch. It would be about nine o'clock in the evening in Australia. He dialled his mother's number.

'We weren't expecting to hear from you so soon, Euan.'

'Has Uncle Simon arrived all right?'

'Of course. He's still quite tired with travelling though. Do you need to speak to him?'

'No. I'd like you to do me a favour.'

'A favour? Whatever can that be?' Euan rarely asked for help, or anything else. At the age of fifteen, he had grown up overnight when news reached them that his father had drowned in a boating accident. He was fiercely independent. 'What can I do for you, dear?'

'I want you to send an email to Uncle

Simon's P.A. It would be better if she believes the instruction is direct from her boss, rather than an order from me.'

'An order, Euan? Don't you mean a request?'

'Well, yes, I suppose so,' he agreed shamefacedly. He was used to giving directions to his own staff and they rarely questioned them, but he was still smarting from his recent confrontation. 'We've rather got off on the wrong foot,' he admitted reluctantly.

'I see.'

'I don't suppose you do. I can't decide whether she's super conscientious or plain stubborn.'

'Or simply not complying with your wishes, eh?' Euan could visualise the gleeful gleam in his mother's blue eyes.

'All I want is for her to take Friday off and accompany me down to Uncle Simon's farm, but she seems to regard visits to Ashburn as a pleasure which she reserves only for weekends and holidays. The trouble is, she is tied up for the next two weekends.'

'Couldn't you find the way yourself?'

'Of course I could, but I'd like her to accompany me tomorrow so that I can get her away from the blasted offices.'

'I see . . . ' Aileen Kennedy pondered, wondering whether Euan was manipulating Simon's P.A. for his own convenience.

'I'll dictate what I want you to say, if you have a pencil handy.'

'All right. What's the woman's name? Is she elderly?'

'Her name is Roseanne Fairfax.' He frowned. 'I'm not sure whether Uncle Simon would address her as Miss Fairfax or as Roseanne. They seem to get on very well. He told me he couldn't manage without her.'

'Roseanne Fairfax? I didn't realise she was old enough to be finished at university. Though of course she must be when I think about it. I suppose she'll be in her mid-twenties now. You say she has joined the firm on a permanent basis? She used to do holiday jobs at the factory to earn

33

money when she was a student. I believe she was always a hard worker. Simon has known her since she was a child.'

'I suppose that accounts for it then.'

'Accounts for what?'

'He can't see any wrong in her. You'd think she was his own daughter or something.'

'Yes, he was very fond of her when Roseanne and her sister were children. Her grandfather's farm neighboured Ashburn, the farm your Uncle Simon bought. They became very good friends in spite of being from different generations, especially after Mr and Mrs Fairfax lost their own son. He died of cancer. He was an accountant; only in his forties. His two wee girls spent most of their holidays with their grandparents. Roseanne loved the animals and the countryside, I remember Simon telling me. Their mother owns a boutique. Julian Fairfax was her accountant. That's how they met, I think. She employed a manageress after she had the children but they were still very young when her husband died and she went back to running the business herself. She would need to make a living of course. I believe she has made quite a success. I know she owns at least two boutiques. Simon used to say she reminded him of a fairy on a Christmas tree — fluff and fripperies on the outside but a firm grip underneath. A woman to command respect, he said.'

'There's nothing fluffy about her daughter,' he said grimly.

'Maybe she takes after her grandfather. I believe he was a shrewd business man. Simon always said he called a spade a spade but people respected him for it and often sought his opinion. I know he helped Simon a great deal when he first went to Ashburn.' She gave a soft laugh. 'He knew nothing about farming. Mr Fairfax taught him whatever he has learned, but he never made much money until Mr Fairfax encouraged him to diversify into meat processing. The old man had enough faith in him to lend him the money to get started. That side of his business seems to have flourished better than either of them anticipated, especially during recent years from what Simon tells me.'

'You never told me all this before.'

'I didn't know you were interested in your relations, or your roots.'

'I've never felt I had any roots.'

'No.' His mother sighed. 'You were so young when you went away to boarding school; then there was university. Since then you've always been on the move because of your work.'

'Where do you feel your roots are, Mother?'

'I came out here as a young wife but after your father died I think I might have returned to Scotland if you hadn't been settled at school and at a crucial period in your education.' She sighed again. 'Simon and I are already doing so much reminiscing it's making me feel homesick for Scotland.'

'Then why don't you come back with Uncle Simon?'

'I'll think about it.'

'At least come for a holiday and see how you feel. His apartment is spacious. You'd like it. There's an unfurnished flat as well. I suspect he planned that for Miss Fairfax but she lives off the premises so I expect he'd let you use it.'

'We'll see. Now, about this email?'

Euan dictated the email, wondering how his uncle would phrase it. His mother had given him plenty to think about.

'You can look at the machinery but don't go worrying the staff,' his uncle had warned. 'They're all good workers. We use best quality products and we've built up a reputation for dependability. We could sell all we produce to two of the top London stores, but I dinnae intend putting all our eggs in one basket. I began selling through the local shops and we'll continue to supply them. We get a bit less per unit but it costs less in transport, and they pay quicker. Roseanne agrees it's the bottom line which counts. I appreciate the loyalty o' ma customers as well as ma workers. Don't forget that, young Euan.' Euan had smiled at his uncle, feeling three years old instead of thirty.

When Euan returned to the meat factory he didn't go near the offices. He donned the regulatory white coat and hat and white wellingtons and spent the rest of the day going round the processing plants. His mind buzzed with improvements if his uncle could be persuaded to install automated machines. He spoke to the workers. They all seemed cheerful and happy. He wondered whether Roseanne had received the email yet and whether she would suspect his manipulation. Maybe it would be wise to wait until morning before facing her. He was living in his uncle's apartment on the top floor above the offices so he decided to go straight up there when he finished looking round the processing plants. He felt unusually restless.

He was surprised to discover a garden and a small area of woodland right at the back of the factory premises where the grounds adjoined the low hills to the west of the town. An elderly man was weeding one of the rose beds and he learned that his uncle had created the garden for the benefit of the staff.

'Some o' them enjoy a walk, or wee seat in the sunshine, during their lunch break, ye ken,' the elderly gardener informed him.

'Yes, I can understand that,' Euan responded. 'You keep it well.'

'Thank ye, young sir, but it's the garden that keeps me going. Mr Kershaw thought it might after I lost my Annie. He has a wise head an' a kindly heart. He strolls around in the evenings when the place is quiet. 'Tis a pity he never took a wife and got himself a son and heir to keep things going. I reckon it's been a great comfort to him though now Miss Roseanne has come back to work here all the time.'

* ★ ★ ★

Roseanne was finishing for the day when the email came through. She was surprised. Mr K rarely sent emails unless they were essential, and surely this couldn't be urgent. Something was not right about it but she couldn't work out what it was. She frowned as she read, but she smiled when she reached the bottom and realised it was from Mrs Kennedy. Mr K was making use of his sister already. Even so it was strange that he considered his nephew needed a guide to drive down to Ashburn, considering he had travelled all over the world without mishap. Surely he was capable of introducing himself to the farm staff, even Jock McIntyre, who could be taciturn if someone got the wrong side of him. Jock had been born at Ashburn and he had risen to herdsman before Mr Kershaw bought the farm following the death of the previous owner. He had continued as dairyman, but he was no longer fit for all the work he had to do — yet he didn't want to retire. On reflection it would be better if he and Euan Kennedy got on together. They might be able to use Euan's expertise if they invested in computerised robots to do the milking but it would be vital to assure Jock his experience with the animals would still be needed.

Roseanne chewed her lower lip thoughtfully. Euan hadn't returned to his office all afternoon so even if he had received a copy of the email too he would not realise there was a change of arrangements for tomorrow. The last Friday of the month was payday so it was always busier than usual. Perhaps if she came in very early she could get through the essential transactions before they set out for Ashburn. It would never do if the wages were not in the workers' accounts by Friday night. It had taken a lot of persuading to convince some of them their money would be safe and paid promptly if it went directly into their own banks. Mr K must have forgotten it was the end of the month but she supposed it was easy to lose track of the days with all that travelling and crossing time lines.

The following morning when she looked out of her window, Roseanne's spirits rose. There had been rain during the night but the sun was rising on the freshly washed world. Across the road the tight buds of the beech hedge were beginning to unfurl and birds were darting hither and thither, already singing their hearts out, mating and building nests. She spent most week-ends at Ashburn except when Robinia was home from one of her many modelling trips. Her sister had never enjoyed the farm. As soon as she was old enough she had helped their mother in her boutique. Even then she had had an eye for colour and stylish clothes.

On reflection she was glad she was going down to the farm, even if it was only for the day, and she was pleased she would be the one to show Euan Kennedy around Ashburn.

Euan was an early riser too and he had been delighted to discover the garden and the little wood which bounded two sides of the grounds. Now he could resume his morning jogging. He was pulling on his jogging pants when he glanced out of the window and saw Roseanne's pale blue car arrive. He admired her trim figure in the navy trouser suit which showed her long legs to advantage. He watched her skip up the steps to the main door as lithe as a schoolgirl. Her clothes were smart and she was always neat. He wondered what she was like away from the office. He was surprised how much he wanted to get her away from the place and spend time with her. He wanted to know all about her. Whoever this Rob was, she was not wearing his ring yet.

An hour later Roseanne sighed when she heard Euan entering the office long before the usual start to the day. He had enjoyed his morning exercise and a refreshing shower. His brown hair was still damp when he put his head round her door.

'You're in early today, Miss Fairfax. Are we overworking you?' She looked at him sharply but there was no trace of mockery.

'Not at all. Have you checked your emails this morning?'

'No, not yet. Is there anything important?'

'No, not important, but I had an email from your mother. I wondered if you'd had one too.'

'My mother?' There was no need to feign surprise. 'Is she . . . ?'

'She's fine. She was writing on behalf of Mr Kershaw. He arrived safely but apparently he's a little travel weary.' She smiled. 'At least that's his excuse this time for having someone else write his emails.'

'I see.' He frowned. 'May I see this email?' He came and stood close behind her. Too close. She was aware of his arm across the back of her chair. She could smell his cologne, or was it aftershave? It was spicy and sharp, attractive. Her fingers fumbled as she saved her document and brought up the list of emails.

He read over her shoulder. She felt his breath against her cheek, warm with a hint of mint.

'I see . . . ' There was relief in his voice. 'Does my uncle send many emails?' he asked curiously.

'He can send them when pushed, but he prefers someone else to do them. I'm sure he finds it an improvement now we have broadband all the time instead of pay as you go. It could be tricky for days like today, paying in all the wages.' She gave a wry smile. 'He will read emails though — when they are meant for him, that is.' He couldn't miss the barb but he remained silent. 'He has taken his laptop so I can keep him up to date while he's away. It's strange because your mother has requested I reply directly to her if there is any reply. I hope he's all right.'

'Probably making use of her as a temporary P.A.'

'Maybe.' She turned slightly, a wary look in her green eyes, but she found his face was so close, her mouth was only a breath away from his. She jerked back. He laughed softly. He knew she was not shy, but she was certainly not the type of woman who threw herself at a man. He found that pleased and intrigued him.

3

Euan straightened, a smile lifting the corners of his mouth. 'Will you be accompanying me to Ashburn after all then?'

'I suppose I must, if I can get peace to finish my work first.' She was relieved to find she could breathe freely again. Why was she so aware of him?

'Surely you could pass the work to one of the other office staff?'

'Not today. I pay the wages direct into their bank accounts at the end of the month.'

'What happens if you are on holiday?'

'I arrange the dates to suit.'

'Very laudable. What if you're off sick?'

'If it was long term your uncle would ask our accountants to handle the wages, as he used to do before I took over.'

'I see.' He eyed her shrewdly. 'You seem to have made yourself indispensable.' His tone was cool now, almost suspicious.

'No one is indispensable, but we have cut down considerably on the accountants' fees since I became . . . since I came to work here permanently. If Mr K relies on me it is because he has no one of his own who has shown any interest,' she added coldly.

'He could have asked for my help.'

'If help is offered he makes use of it if he needs it, but he's too proud to ask for it. Anyway, you're too far away in America.'

'So you offered your help?'

'I didn't need to. We have a business arrangement. When I finished university your uncle offered me a job reorganising the administration side. The processing was expanding and he couldn't keep up with everything. I enjoy a challenge, and the responsibility too, I suppose. Gradually he passed on more confidential matters. I do a

48

good job for which I am well rewarded.'

'I'm sure you see to that all right when you pay your own wages.'

'My remuneration is paid by the firm's accountants, as is your uncle's,' Roseanne said, gritting her teeth at his innuendoes. 'Now if you're expecting me to accompany you to Ashburn today . . . '

'Okay, okay. Eleven o'clock prompt?'

She wondered what he would say if he discovered she was a partner in Kershaw & Co. She supposed if his uncle had considered it any of his business he would have told him, although she was the one who had insisted none of the staff should know there had been any changes. Her grandfather had loaned Simon Kershaw the money to start up the processing company. Before his death he had discussed his affairs with her mother. They had agreed he would leave the farm to Roseanne on the understanding her mother would leave Robinia the two

49

boutiques which she owned outright, as well as a third boutique on which she held a long lease.

It had been a surprise to Roseanne to discover she would also inherit the capital he had invested in Kershaw & Company. She had had a responsible position by then, and Simon Kershaw was already in the habit of discussing ideas and projects for the company with her. She was interested in his plans and the developments, so she had elected to leave her money in the firm in return for a percentage of the profits, as her grandfather had done. Simon Kershaw had been relieved to know she shared her grandfather's faith in him. He had wanted to announce to the staff that she was now a partner.

'I'd rather you didn't,' she said. 'I've worked with most of them during my vacations and I think I have a good relationship with them all. I don't want to spoil it. Anyway there's only room for one boss in a small company.'

Mr K had demurred at first, but he

had seen her point of view. 'Aye lassie, you may be right. You gained some valuable experience when you were here as a student. I've noticed even the older workers come to you to sort out their problems.'

She enjoyed the challenges of the expanding company, or she had until Euan Kennedy arrived. He had an air of authority that was hard to ignore but there was no denying he had a certain charisma. Her mother believed she had all the brains and ice in her veins, while Robinia had all the fire in her veins and an empty head. This was certainly not true, even though Robinia did act frivolously and enjoyed drifting in and out of relationships. They shared the same vibrant colouring and neat features but it was Robinia's job to look good and to be admired. At work Roseanne tried to be neat and well-groomed because she felt her appearance would inspire confidence in her ability. Her cool demeanour also helped keep unwanted male attentions at bay, so the fact that Euan Kennedy's dark good looks were disturbing her equanimity was a new experience for Roseanne.

Promptly at eleven o'clock, Euan appeared in her office as she was tidying her desk and filing away some papers. 'Ready?' He had changed into a blue open-necked shirt and jeans. He looked tanned and fit and Roseanne wished her heart wouldn't lurch so.

'I'm almost ready. Give me a minute to leave a couple of letters for Louise to do and I must ask Hannah to finish my filing. I shall blame you if they grumble at having extra work on a Friday,' she added, reminding him he had meddled with her plans.

'That's all right. I've a thick skin and I'm sure it will be worth it.'

'Right,' she said, gathering up her purse, 'I'm ready.' She followed him down the corridor to the outer door.

'Will you follow in your car?'

'We're driving down together in mine.'

'But I shall need mine to get back here.'

'I'll bring you back.' He was hoping to persuade her to stay longer but he had no intention of telling her so right now. 'You'll want to go home to change? I'll follow you home then . . . '

'No, I'm going as I am.' She frowned. 'But I still think I should take my car in case you decide . . . '

'In case nothing. Your car will be safe here until you return. Come on, jump in.' Roseanne eyed the sleek lines of his sports car.

'Are we travelling with the hood up or down?'

'Better leave it up. It might rain.'

'Mmm, I doubt it,' she murmured, glancing up at the scudding clouds. 'I think there's too much wind, but it might come later.' She removed her jacket, folded it neatly and laid it on top of his overnight bag before stretching her arms above her head and flexing her fingers, her head thrown back, revelling in the fresh air. She gave a joyous laugh and Euan couldn't take his eyes off her.

'I always enjoy escaping to Ashburn to be re-energised,' she explained when she saw his eyebrows raised in question. She smiled down at him then climbed in beside him with a graceful folding of her long legs.

'You should have been a dancer,' he remarked.

'Oh no.' She grinned, shaking her head. 'Mother sent us for dancing lessons, piano lessons, skating, horse riding — anything she considered young ladies might be required to do.' She chuckled; a soft, warm sound. 'I'm afraid I was a disappointment on that front. I always preferred the horse-riding and staying with my grandparents. My sister was the dancer. She won lots of competitions when we were young.'

Euan realised he was already seeing a different side to Miss Fairfax. This was a relaxed Roseanne, as though she had cast off a restrictive skin along with her jacket. He looked forward to the day with even more anticipation. He had known lots of glamorous women, and lots of hard-boiled businesswomen, but he had not encountered any as complex as Roseanne Fairfax appeared to be. He had a feeling she was going to prove a challenge he might find impossible to resist.

He was a good driver, fast but safe, Rosanne admitted. 'We've made good time today,' she said. 'We should stop for a meal in Lockerbie and buy some provisions for you for the weekend.'

'I brought some of our own products — sausages, bacon, a steak pie.'

'I know. I phoned through to Eileen, in the packaging department. We always take some of our own stuff.'

'We?'

'Your Uncle often comes too if he's free.' She frowned, recalling Eileen's teasing about spending the weekend with an attractive young man for a change, instead of being a companion to his uncle. Her reply had been sharper than she'd intended but she hoped it had put an end to Eileen's romantic speculations.

'So what else do we need?' Euan asked.

'Fresh vegetables to go with the steak pie. Bread. If you turn off at the next junction we could get lunch at the hotel before we go into the town.'

'If you say so, ma'am. Does that mean you'll cook us an evening meal?'

'I'll cook a meal before I leave, but you'll need food to fend for yourself tomorrow and Sunday. If you run me back into Lockerbie tomorrow morning I could catch the early train. Mrs Lennox will be terribly vexed she's missed you.'

'There'll be plenty of weekends to meet Mrs Lennox. We'll travel back together,' he announced firmly. 'That's what we agreed.'

'On the contrary — you suggested, but I don't remember agreeing to anything. If it's too much trouble, tomorrow morning, Jock McIntyre will run me to the station, or William, his grandson, if he's around.'

'How old is he and does he work at the farm, this fellow William?'

'He's nearly eighteen. He's doing exceptionally well at school. His parents want him to go to university but he loves the farm and the animals, so he spends all his spare time helping his grandfather. We ... he gets paid for helping out with seasonal work or with the winter feeding. They use a feeder wagon which weighs the various ingredients, such as silage and cereals and minerals, to make a balanced ration. It's all mixed together automatically in the wagon, then they drive down the feed passage and the machine spouts the feed out for the cattle. The animals eat it through a barrier. Jock McIntyre is getting too old to manoeuvre big machines but William has a knack for it.' She sighed and frowned a little. 'Jock doesn't want to retire but he's going to miss William more than he realises if he does go to university. There will have to be some changes. We shall have to reach a decision when Mr K returns.'

'So he discusses the running of the farm with you as well as the processing plant?'

'I've always known about the farm. Grandfather and Mr Kershaw often joined forces and worked the two farms together, helping each other with harvest and silage and things like that. I wanted to go to agricultural college but for once Grandfather agreed with my mother. They decided a degree in accountancy and economics would be more useful for earning my living. They were probably right. After Grandfather died I sold the house and buildings and a small paddock. Neither farm was big enough for modern farming methods with bigger, more expensive machinery, so we run it as one unit.'

'I see . . . So half the land is yours? I had no idea.'

'I think Grandfather would have agreed it is the best solution. The milk is sold to the creamery but everything else is bought and processed by Kershaw & Company.'

'Even the rare breeds?'

'Especially them, or at least the progeny. That's how your uncle started the processing business. He discovered a niche market for traditional meats. It was all done locally at first, but when it began to pay better than his farm he needed to expand. He bought a small factory. It was run down, but it had plenty of land attached and it was nearer to the labour force and to a good road and rail network. He built new premises and gradually expanded. He wanted to live on the premises so his most recent building incorporated his flat. The farm is more of a hobby to him now, but I love it. If I had to choose between them it would have to be the farm.'

'I see,' Euan repeated, but he was frowning. Something was bothering him.

'I don't suppose you do see.' Roseanne smiled. 'How could you when you're a townie and from the other side of the world. I wish your uncle had been here to explain.'

'What else is there to explain?'

'Nothing that need concern you I suppose, though I am hoping you'll . . . ' She broke off. 'Never mind that for now,' she muttered as though impatient with herself. 'Did Mr K tell you I have my own half of the house?'

'He barely mentioned the farm. There was no time. He was flying out almost as I flew in. It seems to me there's a lot of things I need to discuss with my uncle.'

'He only discusses the subjects he chooses to share,' Roseanne warned. 'He's a very private person but he has a forceful personality. He's always kind and fair with his workers though. He insisted I should make my part of the house at Ashburn exactly how I wanted it. He understood I wanted to keep some of the pieces from my grandparents' house. My sister and my mother like everything light and modern. They have no time for sentiment and no interest in old fashioned furnishings.'

'I suppose you keep clothes here as well then? I wondered how you travelled so light. Most women need two suitcases even for an overnight stay.'

'That tells me a lot about the kind of women you choose for company.' She grinned impishly. 'Half my wardrobe is here. The shabby half. My mother and sister disown me in the clothes I wear when I'm at the farm. You're welcome to do the same,' she with an airy wave of her arm.

'I can't picture you ever looking shabby. I'm beginning to think you are two personalities in the same skin, Roseanne Fairfax, like a chameleon. I'm looking forward to getting to know the other side of you. I suspect my uncle is not the only one with a forceful personality.'

'I doubt if you'll approve of this side of me any more than my mother does but frankly I don't give a damn.' She gave him a steady look and he couldn't miss the challenging gleam in her green eyes. His heart beat quickened. She was letting him know she was her own person. 'I come here to relax, recharge my batteries. And,' she added, 'I enjoy myself.'

'Do I detect a warning?'

'If you try to interfere, or tell tales when we're back in the office, then yes. I have an image to maintain when I'm at work.'

'Will there be any tales to tell after we have spent the weekend together, do you suppose?'

'I told you, I'm only here for the day, or until tomorrow morning at most.'

Jock McIntyre was crossing the farmyard on his way to the milking parlour when they arrived. He stopped and stared at the unfamiliar sports car. Roseanne climbed out.

'Well! Hello lassie.' The lined, leathery face creased in a smile. 'Mrs Lennox said you werenae coming down the next two weekends. She said you'd be busy moving house.'

'Yes, I ought to be, but I'm going back to start packing tomorrow. I came down to introduce Mr Kershaw's nephew from Australia.' She turned, beckoning Euan forward.

Jock McIntyre shook Euan's hand vigorously. 'I'm pleased to meet any kin o' Mr Kershaw's.' He pushed back his cap and scratched his head, frowning slightly, then his brow cleared. 'Aye, I remember now. I saw ye once when ye were a wee nipper about this size.' He held his hand two feet from the ground. His blue eyes inspected Euan. 'Your mother brought ye. Mr Kershaw had only just bought Ashburn. She wanted to see it before she went back to Australia to join your father.'

'I don't remember that,' Euan said.

'Ye've never been back until now.' It was more a statement than a question.

'No, I'm afraid I haven't.'

'Mistress Lennox isnae here. She will be vexed to miss ye.'

'None of us knew Mr Kennedy was

coming to Scotland, Jock, not even Uncle K,' Roseanne said. 'Anyway, Mrs Lennox deserved a break and Euan will be here for three months, so he may well be down at Ashburn again.' She glanced at Euan and he saw the laughter in her eyes. 'Unless we scunner him with one visit to the Scottish countryside of course.'

'Och, surely not,' Jock said, cocking an eyebrow at Euan.

'Scunner?' Euan asked.

'It's a good Scottish word. It means if we make you dislike things so much you'll not want to come back,' Roseanne explained with a grin.

'Shall I tell William ye'll be exercising Bella in the morning before ye leave?' Jock asked.

'Yes, please do that Jock. I'll be out by seven as usual in case he wants to exercise Saturn at the same time. Now I'm going to change into my old clothes. Do you want to see the house or shall I leave you with Jock, Mr Kennedy?'

'I'd like Jock to show me round if he has time. I can see the house later.' He caught her arm as she turned away. 'And you know damned well my name is Euan, and that applies to everyone around here,' he added, looking Jock in the eye.

'Whatever ye say, laddie. We dinnae stand on ceremony. I'll introduce ye to Eric, our tractor man, and Donald, who helps with anything and everything.'

'I'll leave you to it then,' Roseanne said and turned to walk to the house, unaware that two pairs of appreciative male eyes followed her all the way.

'Aye, she's a fine lassie, an' no mistake,' Jock said, grinning knowingly as he noted Euan's admiring gaze. 'She'll make a grand wife for some man.'

'I believe there's one in the wings,' Euan remarked casually.

'In the wings, eh? Aye well a man might need wings to catch Miss Roseanne. I havenae heard o' her being swept off her feet yet though. She'll need a man wi' more than milk in his veins if he's to match the fire in hers I reckon.'

Before he left Jock McIntyre to get on with his milking, Euan made sure he understood Roseanne's routine of riding before breakfast.

'And is Saturn my uncle's horse?' he asked Jock.

'He is. If William isnae here she exercises him too when your uncle cannae come down. They often ride together though. Saturn takes a wee bit o' handling,' he added, guessing Euan's intention.

'I think I shall manage him,' Euan assured him, 'though it's some time since I've ridden so I expect I shall pay for the pleasure with some stiff joints.' He grinned.

'Aye. I take it ye'll be riding with Rosie in the morning then?'

'Yes, but I'd like to surprise her. She has me down as a townie but she doesn't know the half of it yet.'

'Ah, like that is it? Well good luck to

ye. I'll tell William to keep out of the way o' the stables in the morning.'

'Does he usually saddle up for Roseanne?'

'Och no, she's done that herself since she could reach her pony's back standing on her wee toes, and she grooms them afterwards. Her grandfather made sure o' that. He brought her up to do things right, even if it did mean hard work.'

★ ★ ★

Roseanne was surprised to find Euan already in the stables when she went down the following morning. He whistled involuntarily when he turned and saw her.

'Stylishly shabby, I'd say!' His eyes travelled unashamedly from her bright yellow polo shirt down to the cream jodhpurs. She raised her eyebrows at his slow perusal and willed herself not to blush. Men had eyed her up before now, but there was something different about Euan Kennedy, and she was not so sure she could deal with him as easily as she usually did. Her hair was no longer coiled around her head. It hung down her back, held in place by a clasp which fitted neatly below her riding hat when she pulled it on.

'Mine's a little big,' he said. 'Is it my uncle's?'

'Ye-es. You intend to ride then? Saturn is not for a novice,' she added anxiously. Whether she was worried about the horse or him Euan couldn't tell; he suspected her concern was mainly for the horse.

'We did a bit of riding at boarding school,' he said, deliberately understating the rigorous lessons they had suffered from an unsympathetic master. Neither did he tell her he had spent some of the school holidays with his best friend, riding with Bob's father and Uncle rounding up the cattle. He remembered the exhilaration and freedom with a feeling of nostalgia. Since his school days he had enjoyed only occasional rides, in the same way that he had taken part in golf, swimming, polo or tennis — all to fit in with clients who wanted to discuss business while taking time for their hobbies. He didn't claim to be an expert in all these things but he had made an effort to attain reasonable standards, quickly realising it was important. Many valuable business agreements had been reached during shared leisure activities.

Roseanne watched him carefully as he mounted the spirited Saturn. Bella was quite spirited herself but she was more easily handled than the larger black horse.

'You lead the way and I'll follow until I get my bearings,' Euan said.

'All right, if you're sure. Shout out though if you're having trouble.'

'Will do,' Euan said, biting back a smile, knowing that his biggest problem would be keeping his eyes off that neat rear of hers in the stretchy cream material. Most women he knew would have expected compliments on their appearance but Roseanne seemed oblivious to her own attractions. His eyes glinted. He intended to make the most of being away from the curious eyes of the Kershaw offices and the wagging tongues in the processing plant. At first they walked slowly along a narrow bridle path, but Roseanne seemed satisfied with his handling of the big black horse and as the path widened she broke into a canter. Eventually they came to a grassy meadow beside the river.

'We'll ride across the meadow today while there's no cattle in and the grass is still short. We don't trample over it when it grows longer for silage.'

'Where do you take the horses for a good gallop if not in here then?'

'At the far side where the river loops there's a little bridge. Usually William and I cross over and let them have a gallop to the top of the hill, then canter down the other side where it's not so steep and come round in a circle.'

'We'll do that then. I think this fellow needs a gallop.'

'We'll gallop to the bridge and I'll wait for you there, see how you feel about going further.'

'Fine,' he said solemnly. He kept Saturn in check behind her but it was clear the horse was used to leading.

'What do you think? Want to turn back?' Roseanne asked as she brought Bella to a gentle halt.

'Could we gallop to the top for Saturn's sake?' he said with a show of humility. 'The last one to reach the top pays a forfeit. How about that?'

Roseanne's eyes widened then sparkled. 'All right. Let's go.'

They clattered across the bridge to where the ground was bare. The horses were obviously used to having their heads on this stretch and for the first half of the hill Euan held Saturn in check, then he let him have his way and they surged forward. Roseanne gasped. Euan had seemed competent enough but he hadn't sounded as confident as all that. She spurred Bella on, but she knew once Saturn was ahead she would never catch him up. At the top Euan sprang from the saddle beneath a clump of trees, grinning triumphantly.

'That was wonderful!' He had a most attractive smile with his white, even teeth and the crinkles around his eyes. Roseanne wondered why she hadn't paid attention before. She slid to the ground beside him.

'I'll tether the horses for a minute or two,' he suggested, 'while I get a look at the view and ... ' His eyes met and held hers; she couldn't miss the wicked gleam even before he added, 'And claim my forfeit of course.'

'F-forfeit?' Roseanne heard herself stammering like a schoolgirl. She'd forgotten about the forfeit. She hadn't expected to be the one to pay.

'We had a bargain. Remember?'

'What sort of forfeit had you in mind?' Roseanne asked, determined to keep her voice even.

'Depends what's on offer.'

'I'll cook you a big breakfast before we leave,' she suggested, knowing they would both be ready for that anyway.

'Mmm, or you could agree to stay until tomorrow morning.'

'I can't do that,' she protested. 'I did warn you. I'll get William to drive me to the train and you can stay . . . '

'That wouldn't be any fun.'

'I didn't realise fun was what you had in mind when you insisted you wanted to see Ashburn. Anyway I must get back, so you'll have to settle for something else,' Roseanne said firmly, aware of the laughter in his eyes and the way they moved over her and came to rest on her face. This was a very different man to the one who had arrogantly taken over Mr Kershaw's office a week ago and whom she had managed to treat with icy disdain since the moment he arrived.

'It'll have to be a kiss then.'

Roseanne stared at him, then she shrugged. Oh well, there was nothing to a kiss. He was probably letting her off lightly. She let out a breath she hadn't known she was holding. Better get it over with. She stepped forward and reached up to plant a kiss on his cheek, but his arms swiftly fastened around her, pressing her close to the whole hard length of him. She gasped.

'I said a kiss,' he growled softly, 'not a peck like an old woman.'

'I . . . ' His mouth came down on hers, silencing whatever words she might have uttered. Her lips were already parted in speech and he took full advantage, moving gently against them, parting them further, taking her by surprise. He deepened the kiss, holding her closer as he did so. She felt powerless to resist. It was a shock to realise she didn't want to stop. Robinia often teased her about being an ice maiden, but she didn't feel so cool now with the blood coursing through her veins. Her sister's words echoed in her memory: 'You're so intense in everything you do, Ros. You'd enjoy making love if only you'd let yourself go.'

'I'll let you know when some man tempts me enough,' she always retorted lightly. Robinia, on the other hand, had been a model since she was in her teens, dressed in everything from ski suits to the briefest bikinis. She had travelled to all sorts of interesting places, and with any number of interesting men. Although she never went into detail, Roseanne knew she had had her fair share of casual affairs.

But casual was not her style and she was intensely aware of Euan's lean body, hard and muscular against her own, and her treacherous response as she felt his arousal. Her knees felt weak, and for the first time in her life Roseanne wanted the kiss to go on — and on.

4

It was Saturn restlessly pawing the ground who brought Roseanne down to earth.

'We'd better get back,' she gasped when she found the strength to draw her mouth away sufficiently to get her breath. Euan released her reluctantly. He was breathing hard. He couldn't remember wanting to make love to a woman as much as he wanted Roseanne Fairfax at that moment.

'Pity,' he sighed, 'but you're right — this time.' He clasped her arm as she turned towards Bella. 'Don't go back today, Roseanne. Please?' He rarely pleaded but he needed time; he longed to explore this side of her. She was so different to the reserved, efficient Miss Fairfax she presented to the world of Kershaw & Co., and even there she intrigued him.

'I must go. We have a busy week ahead at work and I have to pack ready for moving next Saturday.'

'We could leave straight after breakfast Sunday morning. We'd be back before lunch. I'll help you to pack. Have you got boxes?'

'Oh yes.' She began to laugh. 'I can't see you packing underwear or folding dresses.'

'Oh I don't know.' He grinned. 'I wouldn't mind seeing your underwear.' His eyes sparkled when he saw the twin flags of colour mount her cheeks. 'Seriously, I'm sure there's other things. I'm a dab hand with books and I could manage the pots and pans and ornaments. Please, Roseanne? You said spending time at the farm re-energises you. Anyway, you haven't shown me the animals yet.' She hesitated, chewing her lower lip. He drew a finger down her cheek and under her chin, lifting her face. 'Or the boundaries.'

'The — the boundaries?' Her green eyes widened.

'To the land.' He grinned, his eyes more blue than grey in the morning sun and glinting with laughter. 'I'm hoping there'll soon not be any other boundaries between us. Please stay?' He looked faintly surprised. 'I've never said please so often in such a short time in my life!' he confessed.

'I admit I do love it here,' Roseanne agreed with a soft sigh. 'All right, we'll stay, but only if you promise we'll leave here by eight thirty in the morning, as soon as we've exercised the horses and had our breakfast.'

'It's a deal.' His spirits soared.

Euan was a little ahead as they cantered back into the yard. The milk tanker had arrived to collect the day's milk. It was an articulated lorry with a long silver body. The driver was experienced but the farm yard had been designed in the days when cows were milked in byres with the dairy adjoining and a stand for the milk churns at the end of the drive. It took several manoeuvres in the confined space to position the monster tanker close enough to the dairy to connect a hosepipe between the farm milk tank and the road tanker so that the milk could be pumped from one to the other. The morning sun shone brightly on the curved expanse of silver metal.

The sudden glitter startled Saturn. He reared in panic, whinnying and pawing the air. Euan was unprepared and Roseanne's heart thundered as he struggled to regain his balance and grip the horse with his knees. She was sure he would be thrown onto the unyielding surface of the concrete yard before he could control the frightened horse. Bella danced sideways, alarmed by her stable mate's reaction, but she was used to Roseanne so it was not too difficult to calm her and turn her around, heading her out of the yard, away from the tanker.

The driver switched off his engine, staring in dismay at the rearing horse, but it was not the noise of his engine which was alarming Saturn, it was the reflection. Jock McIntyre stood motionless at the dairy door. Roseanne screwed her eyes shut but she couldn't not look. Horse and rider warred with each other. Euan's knees were locked against the sweating Saturn, but he stayed in the saddle and managed to turn the big strong horse towards the yard entrance where Roseanne waited with Bella. Saturn galloped straight past them, over a hedge and across the field without a pause.

The panic was over in minutes, but it seemed an age to the anxious watchers. Euan rode back slowly across the field towards them, unwilling to admit how much his knees were trembling as he slid to the ground and leaned on the gate where Roseanne and Bella were waiting.

'My word, laddie, ye handled that well,' Jock said with relief as he joined them. 'Ye're no novice on a horse, that's for sure. The horses aren't usually in the yard when the milk tanker comes but the driver is early this morning.

He's going to a wedding. And . . . ' His eyes moved from Euan to Roseanne. 'And maybe ye took a bit longer ride than usual, eh?' He grinned when he saw Roseanne's colour rise. 'That's better lassie. Ye looked like a wee ghost before, but ye neednae worry, Saturn knows he's met his master.'

'It was a near thing I must admit,' Euan said, glancing at Roseanne. 'He took me by surprise.'

'We'll wait here until the tanker has collected the milk and departed before we lead the horses back to the stables,' she said. 'Your uncle would never forgive me if I allowed you to get injured on your first day here. We'll take no more chances.'

'It's not the first time ye've ridden a spirited horse though, is it?' Jock said knowingly. 'I dinnae think ye need worry about him lassie. He's a man who can look after himself, if I'm not mistaken.' He grinned and strode back to the dairy. Roseanne's eyes followed him. She nodded slowly.

'You misled me about your riding experience, Euan Kennedy,' she said accusingly, fixing him with that steady green gaze, and he knew she was thinking as much about the forfeit he had demanded as about the near catastrophe.

'I learned to ride at boarding school and we had a pretty tough teacher, but for a minute or two I was not so sure I could control Saturn and stay on his back.' He turned and patted the horse's neck. 'I'll groom them if you like, while you cook breakfast.'

'No, I'll see to Bella then I'll cook breakfast while you soak in the bath. It will help to ease your muscles if you haven't ridden for a while.'

'That's considerate of you. Dare I hope you're offering to scrub my back as well?' he asked, his eyes dancing.

'Don't push your luck!' Roseanne muttered, but she couldn't prevent the tell-tale colour staining her cheeks at the thought of Euan in the bath. He chuckled as though he had read her mind.

They enjoyed a hearty breakfast and Euan helped clear the dishes.

'I didn't have you down for the domesticated type,' she told him frankly.

'We have a lot to learn about each other, I guess. I don't get much opportunity to be domesticated. I do a lot of travelling. I've built up a company and a good team but there's a price to pay for success. Before Uncle Simon telephoned to say he was going to Australia to visit my mother I had been toying with going back there and staying in one place for a while. When I knew Mother would have company I thought it would make a change to spend some of the time in Scotland instead. A man can get tired of living in hotels, however comfortable they may be. This . . . ' He allowed his gaze to roam around the large sunny kitchen. ' . . . is more like home. Sometimes I'd sell my soul for a plate of creamy scrambled eggs, or homemade strawberry jam with newly baked bread. You don't get that sort of choice when

83

you're continually moving around.'

'No, I suppose not.'

He was standing close beside her and he had changed into slim-fitting jeans and a white open-necked shirt which showed off the tanned column of his throat down to the first fuzz of dark hairs on his chest. She glanced up and blushed when she found his eyes on her and an amused smile curving the corners of his mouth. He quirked an eyebrow.

'Takes some getting used to.'

'Wh-what does?'

'Seeing the efficient and immaculate Miss Kershaw as a blushing maiden in skin-tight jeans and — '

'They're not skin-tight! They're — '

'Oh I'm not complaining.' He grinned. 'I just can't take my eyes off them, especially the worn patches on your thighs and around here.' He patted her derrière, then jumped out of reach, grinning as she swiped out with the dishcloth.

'You'd better watch your step or I

'shall be taking the next train back,' she warned, but her eyes were sparkling.

They spent a companionable morning looking round the animals, particularly Mr K's specials, which were either rare or more uncommon breeds.

'This is almost like a farmstead on its own,' Euan reflected as they entered a square shaped yard with stone buildings all the way round.

'It was the old original farmstead. The two areas can be separated for working with the beef cattle by the long iron gates at the top side of the house. They're not as docile as the dairy cows. The stables and the big cubicle shed where the cows sleep, the dairy and milking parlour were all built shortly before your uncle bought Ashburn. That's a long time ago now and the parlour was never meant for milking a hundred and twenty Jersey cows.' She turned to look at him and her eyes were thoughtful.

'Come on Roseanne, out with it. Were you going to tell me my uncle has not moved with the times? I've already guessed that as far as the factory is concerned.'

'I was not going to criticise. The farm still makes a profit, but it could make more. I was thinking about the workers. Jock is well over sixty and Mr Lennox is heading that way, so there will be changes whether we like it or not. There are so many modern aids now in farming as well as in other industries, but most of them need people who understand them, as well as being good stockmen. Did you know there are robots to do the milking now? The cows come to the stalls when they want to be fed their cake and get milked. Each one has a number so it gets the correct allocation of cake, controlled by a computer which can be set according to the yield of milk the cow gives.'

'Are you pulling my leg?' He stopped walking and took hold of her shoulders, frowning at her upturned face.

'Of course not! I'm serious. Honestly. Robots aren't common yet, but you ought to know about such things. I thought they were more in your line of work, being as they're operated by computers. You have to train the cows to come in to them of course, but I'm told they learn very quickly.'

He looked at her, still sceptical. 'For a start I should think it's impossible to train cows like that to come and get themselves milked.'

'Of course it isn't,' Roseanne argued. 'When the cows were milked in byres they all had their own stalls and they never forgot which was theirs. If you watch the herd now you will see there's always a leader cow and an order of precedence amongst them, and most of them have a preference for which side they like to stand in the milking parlour to have the milking machine put on.'

'Honestly?' He looked at her suspiciously. 'You're not trying to make an idiot of me, are you? Because if you are, Roseanne Fairfax I shall — '

'Truthfully,' Roseanne said hurriedly. 'I'm telling you the facts. This is too important to me to risk sending you up a gum tree.'

'So you admit you might tease me about something of less importance?'

'I might.' She chuckled and her green eyes danced. She sobered. 'Robots are still very expensive. I haven't mentioned them to your uncle, nor discussed modernising the existing parlour, but we shall have to consider changes before long. Younger workers want modern working conditions. It is proving difficult enough persuading him we ought to mechanise the labelling and packaging lines at Kershaw & Co., but that is a priority now we're producing larger quantities and there are so many regulations about listing ingredients. I think he is coming round to the idea.'

'So was it your idea to send for me?'

'No, I didn't know anything about you until Mr K mentioned he had a nephew who was supposed to be a whiz with computers.'

'*Supposed* to be, eh?' Euan grinned.

'Is that what he said? Still, he hasn't seen me since I was a toddler, and Mother doesn't really understand much about my work.'

'Well,' Roseanne said with a shrug, 'let's hope Mr K will listen to your advice for the factory.'

'I'll try to persuade him. But first, tell me more about the use of computers on the farm.'

'I'd like to see some of the robots working myself before planning any changes. They require a lot of capital so we can't afford to make mistakes. We already have computers for feeding the cows as they come into the milking parlour. Ours have collars which identify them as they pass, so they get the right amount of cake according to the quantity of milk they're producing. Eventually they will probably have a chip inserted under the skin to identify them. I haven't shown you the farm office yet, but we have a computer in there too. All the milk yields are recorded in the parlour and transferred back to it.'

'That's interesting. I shall look forward to seeing the milking parlour in operation.'

'Mr Lennox is a working manager so he keeps a record of all the births, or any deaths, for all the cattle, not just the dairy herd. They all have a passport, you see.'

'A passport?' he echoed incredulously. His eyes narrowed in suspicion.

'It's true, I'm not teasing you. When I come down at weekends I register each newborn calf and the information goes to a central government computer in England. It's the law. They issue a passport with our herd number and a unique number for each bovine animal. It looks like a chequebook. If an animal is sold, the correct paperwork must go with it and the central computer has to be notified. Once it's registered, a calf can't even die without the relevant papers. It's called traceability. We get regular checks from officials. It must cost a fortune to pay all the civil servants. I have to be here when they come. Neither Mr Lennox nor Jock understands the computer records, but I'm hoping to teach William. The British government keeps more tabs on the identity of cattle than on human beings,' she said wryly.

'I'd no idea. Is Mr Lennox the husband of Mrs Lennox the house-keeper?'

'Yes. They don't go away often. I don't know what we shall do when they retire, or how we shall replace Jock either, unless we modernise a bit.'

'Mmm, I see what you mean about it taking quite a lot of capital.'

'Yes. We shall need to take it one step at a time. Modernising the processing plants must have first priority.'

'So Mr and Mrs Lennox don't live in the farmhouse?'

'No. Their house is on the roadside. We passed it as we turned into the farm yard.'

'Good, I'm relieved to hear that.'

'Mrs Lennox cooks for your uncle if

I'm not here. She does his washing and keeps the freezer stocked for us. She'll probably do the same for you if you come again when she's at home.'

'I certainly hope to come again.'

'I didn't have you down as a country person, but I don't see why it matters to you whether Mr and Mrs Lennox live in the farmhouse or not, for all the time you're likely to be here.'

'Don't you?'

'No.'

'I think it might one of these days. I don't relish having a chaperone.' He chuckled when he saw her blush. 'Though I suppose your Rob would prefer you to have a chaperone.' He was watching her face carefully and he could have sworn she'd forgotten all about her erstwhile boyfriend.

'A chaperone will not make the slightest difference to me,' Roseanne insisted.

'If you say so.' His eyes glinted merrily. 'But don't say I didn't warn you when I prove you wrong.'

'I wouldn't count on that,' she retorted with more assurance than she felt, considering how readily she had responded to his kiss. She couldn't understand herself acting so out of character.

5

'You'll need to explain about these other animals,' Euan said when they reached the stone built pens in the original old farm yard. 'Some of them look . . . well, different.'

'These are the Gloucester Old Spot pigs.' They leaned over the door of the piggery and watched nine piglets all suckling their mother while she grunted contentedly. Euan was standing close, his arm brushing against hers and he was tempted to put it round her shoulders and draw her closer, but for the first time in his experience he was unsure how this particular woman would react. Most of the girls he had known had welcomed a kiss and a cuddle, but he sensed he must proceed more cautiously with Roseanne.

'The young pigs next door are ready

for weaning, and the two further on will farrow soon,' Roseanne said. 'These ginger hairy ones are Tamworths.'

'They're the same colour as you,' Euan teased. 'Shall I call you Tammy in future?'

'No you will not! Anyway I'm not as ginger as that.'

'Maybe not quite.' There was laughter in his eyes. 'You have beautiful hair with all those golden lights in it and it looks like spun silk, but I'll wager you have a more fiery temper than the ginger pigs.'

'It's the animals you're supposed to be learning about, not me,' Roseanne reminded him. 'The ones at the end are Welsh Saddlebacks. Your uncle prefers to keep them all pure. We label the products accordingly. We're very proud of the natural flavour we achieve and we never bulk up any of our products by adding water or salt. The gammon steaks are delicious. You should bring one with you next week if you come down on your own.' Roseanne knew she was chattering. Was it because he was so close that she felt like an inexperienced teenager?

'It will not be nearly so interesting without you.'

'Your uncle knows I enjoy being here on any pretext, but I still can't understand why he sent that email asking me to accompany you. Maybe he was afraid you'd ruffle Jock McIntyre's feathers.'

Euan ignored her speculation. He wondered how she would react if she discovered he had tricked her into spending this weekend with him. More to the point, what would the boyfriend, Rob, have to say, considering there was only the two of them alone in the house, even if it was a large one? He walked beside her as they crossed to the other side of the yard.

'This looks as though it has been a house,' he remarked.

'It was the original farm house long before our time — a single-storey cottage. Your uncle converted it into two hen houses with fenced runs at the back so they stay separate. These reddish ones are Marans. They lay lovely brown eggs. The others are Light Sussex. Most of the eggs are sold locally from the village shop. We could sell more but we use a lot at the processing plant.

'There's a burn at the back of the buildings. Your uncle dammed it to create a small pond so he could keep some Muscovy ducks, and I'm not sure what the brown ones are.' She shook her head and smiled ruefully. 'They're not at all commercial, but he gets a lot of pleasure out of them and his enthusiasm is infectious. We have so many breeds of animal we could make it an open farm. It would be another source of revenue, we could charge the public an entrance fee to look around — but then we'd need extra staff and public liability insurance, plus more attractions for children. One of us would need to live here to oversee everything.'

She sighed. 'I could make it a good wee business in its own right. The beef cattle and sheep are in the fields at this side of the old steading. If the winter is very severe they can get into these open fold-yards for shelter with hay or silage to supplement the grass.'

'I can see the farm does mean a lot to you, Roseanne, and you understand everything about it.' There was respect in Euan's voice.

'I ought to do. I've been coming down here since before I could walk. Grandfather used to perch me on his shoulders to take me to look at his animals. He was disappointed when my father didn't follow in his footsteps. After he bought Ashburn your uncle often joined us in the evenings, back when Granny was alive. She kept open house. After she died your uncle still came most evenings until he started the meat processing. Grandfather appreciated his company.'

'I imagine it was mutual. My mother told me your grandfather taught Uncle

Simon everything he knows about farming.'

'I don't know about that, but he's an expert at buying top quality animals for Kershaw & Co., whether at the markets or privately. He has placed orders with several of the farmers to keep us supplied while he is away. That was the only thing which worried me about him being away so long. He left me the names of two men he feels I could trust to augment our supplies if I think we might run short.'

'You have more responsibility than I realised.'

'I expect I'll cope.' She shrugged. She felt less comfortable discussing the processing business. If his uncle had wanted him to know she owned almost half the company he would have told Euan himself. Although he was Simon Kershaw's nephew they were almost strangers, and in any case they had had so little time to discuss anything. She didn't like the idea that Euan could check all the transactions through the central computer though. Surely his uncle had never anticipated that. There were one or two personal items which went through the firm's accounts.

'Something troubling you, Roseanne?' Euan asked.

'No, no of course not. We'll walk beside the burn, shall we? It goes along three sides of the paddocks where we rear the beef and lamb. It floods sometimes so we never plough Burnside Meadow. See the big yellow flowers? I often got wet feet trying to pick them when I was small. Granny always gave me a scolding. They're called kingcups. The little ones are buttercups, and of course you'll recognise the daisies.'

'And the dainty lavender-coloured flowers, what are they?'

'They're milkmaids — or at least that's what I've always called them.'

'You really do love the countryside, don't you, Roseanne?'

'Yes, I dream of living down here someday. After lunch we'll walk round the boundaries, if you're not too stiff after your morning ride. I'll show you where my grandparents lived.'

'I'd like that. What are those hairy-looking cattle that look as though they're wearing a white saddle?'

'They're Belted Galloways. The smaller, black ones are Aberdeen Angus — excellent meat but not so hardy. You'll recognise the Highland cattle with their huge horns of course.'

'Yes, they look lethal.'

'They're usually fairly quiet unless they have a new calf. The red and white cattle in the far field are Herefords. We keep more of them. Your uncle believes they make the tastiest beef but they have been replaced by imported breeds like the Belgian Blues, Simmentals and British Blonds. They seem to have pushed many of our traditional British breeds aside. Oh look, there's William.' She waved towards the young man who had been inspecting the sheep in the fields further away. He came towards them with a collie dog at his heels. They met him at the gate.

'William, this is Euan Kennedy. He's a nephew of Mr K. He's a computer expert so he may be able to advise you about your laptop.' She grinned mischievously up at Euan. 'We may as well make good use of your expertise while you're here. This is Jock's grandson, William McIntyre. Are you looking over the stock while Mr Lennox and his wife are on holiday?'

'Yes. I volunteered to count them. Mr Lennox gave me a note of the numbers in each of the paddocks. They're all there and okay.'

'Is there any reason why they shouldn't be?' Euan asked, puzzled, thinking how seldom the huge flocks of Australian sheep could be counted when they were spread over vast areas.

'We always count and check them every day but there's been some cattle rustling in the area,' William explained. 'Or rather, sheep-stealing is the most recent.'

'And you never know with animals.

One could get caught in a fence or take ill and die if they're not checked regularly,' Roseanne added.

'I've decided what I'm going to do when I finish school, Roseanne,' William said. 'I'll be leaving in another four weeks. I've had interviews with the careers advisor and he's got me in for a place at agricultural college to do a Higher Diploma. He reckons I can go on to university and upgrade to a degree if I decide I want that.'

'You're sticking with agriculture rather than computers or accountancy then?' Roseanne asked with a smile.

'Yes. I know I'll never be able to have a farm of my own but this is what I love.' He waved an arm, encompassing the fields and animals.

'You're a wise young fellow to follow your heart,' Euan said with feeling.

'Is that what you did?' Roseanne asked curiously.

'I haven't followed my heart yet,' he said gravely, 'but I'm hoping it's not too late. The truth is, William, you're lucky.

You know what you want to do. I didn't have a clue. I was good at maths and science. I considered engineering but I drifted into computer programming. I spent a frustrating two years in a firm where other guys used my ideas and took the credit. I had no ties so I decided to set up on my own. Mother was worried sick, but at twenty-two I suppose I was rash and conceited. I'd nothing to lose and I was prepared to work hard. I've been lucky. Things took off. I'm thirty now and I could almost afford to retire if I sold my company, but I've never had time to relax. I could never idle my time away doing nothing but I feel I'm missing out on some of the more important aspects of life. During the next three months I shall take stock and see which way the future beckons.'

'So you don't think I'm crazy then, Mr Kennedy, even though you've made your fortune?' William asked earnestly. 'Mum and Dad think I ought to study accountancy like Roseanne.'

'Whatever you decide, William, I think there's a price to pay. In your case you may not earn as much money as you would like, but you'll probably be satisfied with your work and happy with your life. In my case the constant travelling and demands pall after a while. There's little time for real friendships when you're always on the move. I'm a hands-on type but I shan't be able to keep up the pace forever.'

Roseanne was amazed. She'd learned more about Euan in the few minutes he talked so frankly to William than she'd learned in a week.

'Thanks.' William grinned suddenly. 'Grandpa keeps telling Mum it's not all gold that glitters. So can I pick your brains about my laptop, and computers in agriculture sometime?'

'Certainly, if you think I can help. We'll talk again next weekend.'

'We're off for some lunch now, but we might walk around the boundaries if Euan is not too exhausted,' Roseanne said with a wink at William. 'He's not used to country living.'

'I still keep myself fit!' Euan said indignantly, then saw her green eyes dancing and William's grin.

Roseanne had taken a carton of Mrs Lennox's cock-a-leekie soup from the freezer for their lunch and she had bought crusty rolls and cheese. 'There's fruit and coffee to finish. Will that do?' she asked.

'This is delicious soup,' Euan said. 'I doubt if I'll have room for the fruit. Maybe we can take an apple in our pockets and find a pleasant spot to sit and eat it when we're walking round the boundaries?'

'Good idea. You still feel up to it then? It's quite a long walk all the way round. We could take the Land Rover if you prefer.'

'No, a walk will be good for us, especially if we're to eat that steak pie and all those vegetables you bought when we return.'

'That was the idea,' Roseanne said with a grin, enjoying his company more than she had thought possible. She believed in first impressions but now she wondered if she had allowed prejudice to cloud her judgement when they first met.

It was a pleasant afternoon for a leisurely walk and Roseanne was pleased at the interest Euan was taking in the countryside and the farm, as well as the general flora and fauna.

'I suppose I should have all sorts of questions if I visited Australia,' she said.

'Am I asking too many questions?' Euan enquired seriously. 'So many things are new to me and seeing everything so lusciously green is wonderful.'

'I'm pleased you're interested. You were asking what the line of hills were to the west. They are the Galloway Hills, and the highest one is Criffell. We use that as a guide to the weather. There's no mist on the top today so we can be pretty sure there'll be no rain before morning. Sometimes you can't see it for mist then rain usually follows.

When we get to the top of the rising ground that's the highest point on Ashburn. On a clear day like today we should be able to get a glimpse of the Solway Firth.'

'Is that the sea? Maybe we could go there one day?'

'I suppose it is the sea in that it is salt water and tidal, but the tide goes a long way out, then there's a large stretch of sand. It's not the same as the ocean. It can be quite dangerous for swimmers when the tide comes in. There was a lot of smuggling at one time.'

They walked in friendly silence until they came to a narrow wood.

'Ashburn boundary is this side of the trees,' she said, 'but if we go through the wood we can look down on Ferniebrae, the house where my grandparents lived.'

He had no difficulty loping over the fence with his long legs, but the fence had been renewed since she last walked the boundary and she needed to climb up the squares of netting. She felt her heartbeat quicken when he turned and scooped her up in his arms and set her down on the other side.

'Goodness, you're stronger than you look!' she gasped, wishing she was not so aware of his male attractions. He didn't release her immediately, but stood smiling down at her pink cheeks.

'You're light as a feather. Come on, I'll keep hold of your hand until we get through the wood. I assume you don't come this way often when there's so many brambles?'

'I haven't been for a long while. It's rougher than I remember. Would you rather turn back? I'd hate you to tear your clothes.'

'I can manage, so long as you're all right.'

'Yes, I'm fine.' She liked the way he tried to trample down or hold back the brambles and nettles to make a safe passage for her. He swore fluently when a long bramble flew back and scratched his hand but he sucked it and continued to make a pathway.

'We're nearly through the wood. Do we have to come back this way?'

'No. The owners won't mind if we go along the edge of the paddock on the other side of the fence. It's a bit further but it'll bring us out at an old track and there's still a gate where we can get back into our own fields.'

There were two elderly ponies in the paddock. They waited until they had climbed over the fence then they ambled slowly towards them.

'They're looking for titbits.' Rose-anne smiled. 'They belonged to the children of the couple who bought the house but they will have outgrown them by now. In fact I think they will both be away at university. If we walk a bit further along the edge of the wood we shall get a good view.'

'There's a house,' Euan said a few minutes later. 'It doesn't look like an old farmhouse from here though.'

'They did a lot of alterations, building on a double garage with two bedrooms and a bathroom above and a large conservatory to the side. They asked me over to see but I wanted to remember it the way it was when Granny was alive. For me it's the people who lived there who made it a home.'

'It would be a happy home again if it was yours, with your children around you.'

'I haven't got any children.'

'Not yet, but I'm seeing a different side to the efficient Miss Fairfax I see at Kershaw's. I can imagine you being happy with a brood of children now I've seen you here. Do you like children, Roseanne?'

'Oh yes, but even if I had any I couldn't afford to buy the house back now. I've invested the money in other things.'

'Like half a farm that doesn't pay as well as it should but makes an elderly man happy?' He quirked an eyebrow and gave her a whimsical smile but he noticed she didn't answer his question.

'We'll walk as far as the end of the

wood, then we'll sit down and eat our apples, shall we?'

'Suits me. Is that an orchard we can see at the side of the house? The trees are coming into blossom.'

'Yes. Granny had apples and pears and a couple of plum trees. She made lovely raspberry jam.'

Euan found it hard to reconcile the wild and happy child he was picturing with the immaculate and efficient Miss Fairfax who confidently took charge of Kershaw and Co. She really was like two different people in the same skin, and he wanted to know all of her. He had never felt so deeply interested in any of the women he had known before.

'I'm glad you have happy memories, Roseanne. No wonder you dream of returning to this area one day. I never knew my grandparents.'

'That's a shame. I treasure the memories of the time I spent with mine but I never knew my maternal grand-parents.'

At the edge of the wood they came to a grassy bank where there were still a few late primroses.

'Shall we sit here a while?' Euan asked.

'Mmm, this will do fine.' Roseanne realised he was still holding her hand. She released it and flung herself face down on the cool grass. 'It's beautifully warm for the time of year,' she said, cradling her head on her arms and turning her face towards him. 'The bluebells should be out by now but there's never been any in this wood. I think I'd plant some if it still belonged to me.'

Euan pulled two apples out of the pockets of his wind cheater and handed her one. She sat up and turned to face him, biting into the crisp flesh with small strong teeth.

'I'm glad we brought them,' Euan said. 'I'm quite peckish now.'

'I thought we might be ready for them,' Roseanne murmured. 'It's further than you think to walk right round now that the land from both farms is joined. I've brought a bar of chocolate in case you were a good boy and deserved a treat.'

'I have been very good. I'm sure you agree.'

'Mmm.' She gave him a considering look, her eyes twinkling. 'You did get wounded protecting me from the brambles so I suppose that has earned you one square. It's a pity the ponies didn't follow us; we could have fed them our apple cores,' she said, throwing hers with considerable force down the field before she pulled out a large bar of chocolate.

'Only one square?' Euan asked with a chuckle. 'I'll wrestle you for the rest of the bar,' he challenged, his grey eyes dancing.

'Oh no you won't, you're bigger than me.' She broke off a row of small squares. She looked at him, her eyes sparkling. She seemed about to feed it to him; he opened his mouth but with a laugh she popped it into her own instead.

'Oh, oh, so that's the way you play your games, Roseanne Fairfax! We'll see about that.' Before she realised what he was about he had rolled over, holding her down with one long muscular leg while he tried to pin her arms above her head.

'Surrender, surrender,' she laughed. 'Here's yours.' She stuffed a chunk of chocolate into his mouth. As he chewed it he seized her other hand and wrested the remainder of the bar from her grasp.

'I'm boss now.' He grinned down at her. 'You can only have another piece if you pay a forfeit.'

'Oh no! I'm not paying any more of your forfeits.'

'Why not?' he asked guilelessly. 'You enjoyed — '

'No I did not! I — '

'Enjoyed that last piece of chocolate, I was going to say.' He feigned a look of innocence. 'But if you didn't enjoy it, I'll eat it myself.' He popped a generous piece into his mouth and then broke off another small square and placed it between her lips. As she sucked it in he placed his mouth gently over hers in a feather-light kiss.

Seconds later he raised his head. 'I've heard of candy kisses but I've never had a chocolate kiss before.' He grinned as he watched the colour rise in her cheeks. 'You blush so beautifully, Roseanne.' He stroked her cheek with a gentle finger. 'Exactly the colour of wild roses. I think your mother made an excellent job of choosing your name.' He broke the remaining chocolate in half and cradled her head in his arm while he fed some to her and some to himself, stealing a playful kiss between each morsel until it was finished.

'That was delicious,' he said.

'Yes, but the chocolate is all done so you can release me now.' Roseanne said, but Euan didn't move. He simply looked down at her, studying her face.

She knew he was going to kiss her and didn't want to resist.

She could taste the chocolate on his

tongue as it toyed with hers.

'Lovely,' he breathed, as though he had read her mind. His lips trailed a line of little kisses down the line of her jaw and back until he nibbled her ear. His mouth claimed hers again, more demanding, deepening the kiss until her legs felt week and she grew hot with desire. No one had ever aroused her like this before. She hadn't known it was possible. He released her hands and she felt his fingers on the bare skin where her shirt had escaped from her jeans. His hand moved slowly in ever widening circles until his fingers found the swell of her breasts. He felt her nipple peaking, firm and hard against his thumb and he lowered his head in a long, exploring kiss.

'No,' she murmured softly as his fingers slipped beneath her bra and she became aware of his increasing desire. 'Not here. Not now. Not yet . . . '

'You're right,' he breathed softly and raised his head to stare down at her swollen lips and flushed face. 'This is not the place to make love to you the way I want to love you, Roseanne.' He rolled away from her and drew his knees up, pushing his fingers through his thick brown hair. Roseanne smoothed her own hair as best she could and then rose to her feet. She looked down at him.

'It will be better tonight. We have the house to ourselves,' he said softly. 'It will be better to have privacy. I should have realised you're not the sort of girl for a quick roll in the grass.'

'No Euan, I don't think you understand. I'm not that sort of girl at all. Not anywhere. We scarcely know each other.'

He stared at her. She was serious. 'You can't mean that. I could swear you were as aroused as I was just now. I feel we've known each other forever . . . '

'After one week? Is that the sort of line you use with all the women you meet on your travels when you're feeling bored?'

'No it is not. I rarely have time for

women in that way, if you must know. You're a very attractive woman, Rose-anne. I can't be the first man to tell you that. And when the housekeeper is away and there's only the two of us . . . '

'You've got it all wrong,' Roseanne said firmly, but in her heart she knew he hadn't.

'Old Jock guessed this morning that I was attracted to you.'

'Jock doesn't know anything of the kind!'

'He guessed I'd kissed you by the way you blushed.'

She scowled because she had seen the twinkle in Jock's eyes too.

'Mm, it surprised me too after my first impressions of the prim and proper Miss Fairfax I've seen all week. Perhaps I should try it again to make sure I've not been dreaming.'

'No, you should not!' Roseanne declared. His grey eyes travelled over her face, coming to rest on her mouth. She saw the desire in them and trembled. She was not afraid of him, she was afraid of herself and her own response. She sought refuge in the ice image she could do so well.

'Are you telling me the reason you wanted me to come down here with you was because you fancied a bit of a fling while you're in Scotland?' she demanded coldly.

'It had never entered my head, but now you mention it I confess that cool, touch-me-not image you present at the office intrigues me.'

'It was not meant to. I'm sure most women are ready to fall into bed with you whenever you beckon. Well, let me tell you, Euan Kennedy, I'm not one of those women.' He was silent for a few moments, digesting what she had said.

'I see,' he said slowly. Suddenly he smiled — not the mocking, angry smile she had expected. His expression was almost tender. True, he seemed surprised, but she thought there was a glimmer of satisfaction in his eyes. To her amazement he hugged her close and then released her.

'We know where we stand now. You need have no fear about being in the house alone with me. I promise to observe the boundaries you have set.' Roseanne stared at him. He looked so sincere she didn't know whether to be glad or sorry. He smiled at her, a sort of whimsical smile, and she couldn't tell what he was thinking. Then he said, 'But it's only fair to warn you I shall try to break down your boundaries. I don't know what kind of man your Rob is, but I do know you don't wear an engagement ring, and you're no more immune to me than I am to you, so I mean to win you fair and square.'

'R-Rob . . . ?' Roseanne stammered before she remembered the email to her sister. Euan gave her a quizzical look. He could have sworn she'd forgotten all about the man who would soon be moving in with her and his spirits rose.

6

They walked in silence, each deep in thought. Roseanne felt confused by the gamut of conflicting emotions Euan had awakened in her. She was used to being in control of a situation, and of her feelings. She felt vulnerable and she didn't like that. She should have resisted when Euan started to kiss her. She had always taken relationships more seriously than her sister, taking time to make friends but keeping those she valued. True, she had lost her virginity at university. In her ignorance, or innocence, it had seemed a prerequisite to being accepted as a fully-fledged student. She had not enjoyed the experience and she was fairly sure her partner hadn't either. Consequently she had rarely been tempted to repeat it — until now. She had vowed then she would never again be influenced by public pressure, or other people's opinions, where her private life was involved. She needed to be a hundred per cent committed. When it came to personal feelings she had always believed she would know what her heart desired. She barely knew Euan, and yet he drew her like a magnet. She would not have believed it was possible to feel so aroused, every nerve firing in response to his kisses.

'You're very quiet, Roseanne,' Euan said at length. 'Don't you trust me?'

'Of course I do. You've given your word.'

'Thank you,' he said quietly. 'We'll forget that little interlude then. Obviously I made a mistake. You said you hardly know me. That goes for both of us — but I would like to know the real Roseanne Fairfax. Do you read or swim or play sports? How do you occupy your leisure hours? I know you enjoy walking and riding and you love the countryside.'

'It takes time to really know a

person,' Roseanne said slowly, 'and you will be going to Australia, or travelling the world again, in a few weeks. We'll probably never see each other again.' Why did that thought make her feel so bleak? 'I would like to know more about your work and the places you have been though.'

'As I told young William, I don't know what my future plans are. It was a shock when I heard Mother had had a major operation. She has always been so healthy and fit. She didn't tell me until it was over. It made me realise how I would I have felt if she had died. I suspect Uncle Simon experienced a similar feeling. We are his only relatives.'

'He has you here now.'

'Yes, but we're strangers. I only know of him through my mother. The same goes for him. I sensed a wariness about him at the airport. It's time we got to know each other. If I'm honest, he spoke of you so warmly I thought you must be his wife, or near enough. Then when I saw you and realised you were so young I decided he spoke of you as though you were a favourite niece. I think, subconsciously, I was probably a little jealous.' He grinned at her. 'Now I know you could probably bewitch the devil himself. I shall have to do some serious thinking before I make any big decisions about my future.'

'Yes, I think you should. We all tend to assume those we love will be there forever, but they're not.'

'No, we both know that,' he said quietly. 'Look, isn't that William getting the cows in for milking? Does that mean we have come right round the boundary to the other side of the farm?'

'Yes, to both. I'll point out the rest of the western boundary from here, and then we'll cut across the field and help William round up the stragglers. Do you see across the next field — there is a line of trees and a wee lane beyond it?'

'Yes. There's a Land Rover going along the lane.'

'That's probably Jock. He'll have

been checking the cows which are due to have calves. He insists on seeing them himself in case any are near their time. I've known him wait up half the night for a heifer having her first calf.'

'He must be conscientious.'

'He is. No amount of computers can replace that sort of experience and dedication. Anyway, we have two fields on the other side of that lane. The burn is the boundary in that direction. When we get back to the farm yard you'll see there are four smallish fields. They're sheltered and close to the steading, so the dairy cows graze there at night. It means they're handy for bringing in for morning milking. Now you'll have a fair idea of Ashburn land but I'm sure none of the neighbours would mind if you strayed into their fields.'

'Good, I wouldn't like any of them pointing their gun at me.'

'They might if you eye up their daughters.' She grinned. 'Come on, we'll help William round up the Jerseys.'

126

'Have you seen the local paper, Rosanne?' William asked as soon as they caught up with him. 'Old Mr Arnold has lost eight of his sheep. He's sure they've been stolen. The police found tyre tracks, in the mud leading from the gate into his top field. They reckon they're from a large vehicle with a trailer.'

'Couldn't they be from the farmer's own trailer?' Euan asked.

'Mr Arnold is over eighty. He uses a haulage contractor if he sends his sheep to market, but he usually sells them privately to Mr Kershaw. He has an ancient Austin but he never drives further than the village shop.'

'That's true,' Roseanne agreed. 'I'll bet the thieves know he's an old man and on his own,' she added angrily. 'He's bound to be upset.'

'Where does he live?' Euan asked.

'It's not far in the Land Rover. He only has a small farm now and his land borders the paddock where we saw the two elderly ponies this afternoon.'

'Aye, that's right,' William said glumly. 'He borders with Ashburn land at that top corner. Grandfather says the thieves are getting too close for comfort. He's hoping they don't hear Mr and Mrs Lennox are away.' He looked at Euan. 'They'd only have to buy a stamp at Lenniethlan post office and Mrs Strang would give them all the news for miles around.'

'She would too,' Roseanne muttered. 'She's a kindly soul but an inveterate gossip.'

'That reminds me, Roseanne. Mrs Strang asked Grandfather to remind you there's a concert next Saturday night to raise funds for the village hall. She's depending on you to sing that duet, 'A Wee Bawbee', with Bill Niven.'

'I can't do that. I shall not be down here next weekend. I'm moving to a bigger flat. I'm borrowing a van on Saturday morning. It's all arranged. Will you be sure and give her my apologies please, William?'

'You're planning to move everything yourself?' Euan asked incredulously.

'Of course. There isn't much heavy stuff. The wardrobes are built in. Not much scope for expressing ones personality in my present home,' she smiled. 'But it's the first place I owned and I've been happy there.'

'I see,' Euan said thoughtfully.

'It's nothing like the one your uncle offered me, but it was my own space.'

'Yes, I can understand your need to get away from the factory and have a life of your own.'

'William, do you think you could show Euan how the milking parlour works? I'm going to check the records in the office.'

'Will do. There's a wee Belted Galloway and a Hereford calf to enter in the computer, as well as two Jerseys. The book with the dates in is in the cupboard next to the dairy. Mr Lennox said you'd know where to find it there.'

'Fine. I'll enter them up, then I'll

start cooking the evening meal. I'd like to drive over to see old Mr Arnold before he goes to bed.'

'I was going to give you a hand peeling the vegetables,' Euan said.

'You were?' Roseanne raised a disbelieving eyebrow.

'Yes!' he insisted. 'Not that I claim to be an expert at peeling carrots . . . '

'There'll be other times when you might need to prove yourself. I'll see you when you've had enough of the milking parlour.' She strode away as the cows turned into the gathering yard, leaving William to take Euan into the parlour to start the milking.

★   ★   ★

'I hope you don't mind me leaving you on your own while I visit Mr Arnold,' Roseanne said after they had finished their evening meal and cleared away. 'There's a friendly wee pub in the village. I could drop you off there if you like?'

'I'd rather come with you. We can take my car.'

'You can come, but don't blame me if you're bored.' Roseanne grinned. 'Mr Arnold likes to talk about the past and he knew both my grandparents. It's quite a rough road up to the farm so I'd prefer to take the Land Rover.'

'Fair enough. I don't mind the odd drink but I'm not a great one for drinking the evening away.'

'If it's not too late, we might call in for a wee while so that I can introduce you to the locals. Then you'll know some of them when you're here on your own if you come down next weekend.'

'Ah, I want to talk to you about that. William tells me they rely on you to sing when they have a concert at the village hall. You must be pretty good.'

'No, I'm not. The hall committee are grateful for anyone and everyone who will do some sort of turn.' She chuckled. 'So long as they don't expect to be paid. You should go next Saturday. Jock will introduce you to the villagers and you could always give a gift for the raffle from your Uncle Simon. He's good at supporting local affairs. You can take one from me too.'

'I have a better suggestion. This van you're hiring — would they let you have it on Friday afternoon or early evening?'

'I'm borrowing a company van, the one Sam Liston uses for collecting stores and other odd jobs. I've already spoken to him.' Roseanne coloured at the sight of his raised dark eyebrows and widening eyes, but then he nodded.

'That's better still,' he said with a smile. Was it a smug smile? Roseanne wondered, frowning a little.

'Better?' She had expected him to quibble about her using the firm's property for personal use while his uncle was away.

'Yes. I'll ask Sam if he can finish with the van by Friday lunchtime. If you come in early again we could both be free by then. I'll help you load it up ready for an early start at your new place on Saturday morning. We should have everything moved by lunch-time, then we can drive down here in time for the concert.'

'Whoa! Steady on. I'm not used to anyone organising my life.' Roseanne frowned at him, feeling she was being swept along on an outgoing tide.

'I'm trying to help.' He grinned ruefully. 'But if I'm honest I would appreciate your company again next weekend. Anyway, the move would be quicker with two of us.'

'Maybe so,' Roseanne said slowly, 'if I just dump all my stuff — but I don't like the idea of coming back on Sunday evening to a muddle of boxes.'

'Knowing your ability to organise, you'll have all the essentials to hand. Better still, we could stay here on Sunday night, leave by six on Monday morning and be at the offices before everybody arrives.'

'Let me think about it. I'm not promising to be here for the concert. I hate letting people down if things don't go to plan.'

'I understand.' He nodded.

'Now, I'd better change. Mr Arnold has old fashioned ideas about women in trousers.'

A few minutes later Euan waited in the hall as she ran lightly down the stairs dressed in a floating skirt in a green paisley pattern and matching top. Roseanne saw his eyebrows shoot up and there was no mistaking the appreciative look as his gaze travelled over her. She felt her colour rise and wished she didn't have such a fair skin.

'Ve-ery attractive,' Euan murmured under his breath, but Roseanne heard him and felt a warm glow.

Old Mr Arnold was delighted to see them. Roseanne shook his hand and kissed his leathery cheek.

'Ah, but ye get bonnier every time I see ye, lassie,' he said, beaming from her to Euan. 'And this is your young man, eh? Come in, come in and take a seat, laddie.'

'No, this is Mr Kershaw's nephew, Euan Kennedy, Mr Arnold.' He was slightly deaf and Roseanne had to speak louder than usual.

'Simon's nephew, ye say? Well that'll be a fine match for the pair o' ye. Ye'll have a wee dram, laddie?' He was already reaching for the glasses and a bottle of whisky. Roseanne opened her mouth to correct his assumptions but Euan shook his head and grinned.

'Let it go,' he said softly. 'It can't do any harm if he wants to weave a bit of romance into life.'

'You don't know what the results might be,' Roseanne said darkly. 'He'll be telling Mrs Clark who comes to clean for him and the whole village will be planning a wedding before you know where you are.'

'Would that be so terrible?' he asked, his grey eyes sparkling with laughter.

'Not for you, maybe. You'll be on your way back to your life. I shall be the one left to disillusion them all.'

'What about you, young Rosie, will

ye take a dram?'

'If I can pour my own!' Rosanne said, seeing the large measure in the glass he had handed Euan. 'Do you have any lemonade? Or water will do.'

'Och lassie, you'll ruin a drop o' good scotch if ye water it down.'

'Yes, but I have to drive home so I'll just have a sip to drink your good health. I don't want the police breathalysing me.'

'You havenae far to go. You're only down the road.' He stopped, frowning, remembering. 'But the police might be looking around. Did ye hear somebody stole eight o' my prime lambs?'

'Yes. I'm really sorry to hear about that. Have they any idea who the thieves might be?'

'No, but they must have an outlet — like hotels, or a butcher, or maybe they send them down in London.'

'Did you hear anything the night they took them?' Roseanne asked.

'No, but I dinnae hear so well these days. Jess there . . . ' He nodded towards the collie dog lying on a rug beside the door, who cocked an ear at the sound of her name then settled down again. 'Her ears are sharp enough. She wakened me up with her barking. I looked out o' the door but we're in a bit of a hollow here at the house and I couldnae see the top fields. I thought I saw lights in the sky though. Jess wanted to run out but I dinnae let her. I was feart she'd get shot if it was poachers. She means everything to me, does Jess. I dinnae ken what I'd do without her.'

'Are the police patrolling the area now they know there are thieves around?' Euan asked.

'Aye, but they'll not get my lambs back. They'll be slaughtered by now,' Mr Arnold said glumly. 'If I'd had hundreds o' sheep I might not have missed them for a week or more. Anyway Rosie, tell me how Simon is and what he's doing these days. He usually buys my spring lambs when they're ready.'

They told him all their news and he reminisced happily about his young days and her grandparents and other neighbours who had come and gone during his lifetime.

'Your sister never enjoyed the farm like you did, Rosie. What is she doing? Is she married?'

'No, not yet. She's still doing the modelling, travels a lot. She gets plenty of work.'

'Queer sort o' life . . . ' he muttered, shaking his head.

He thanked them several times for coming when they rose to take their leave.

'Be sure to come again,' he repeated, as he saw them to the Land Rover.

'I'm glad we called,' Roseanne said. 'It's terrible that the thieves have got away with an old man's livelihood.'

'Yes. I'm pleased you let me accompany you. I enjoyed hearing about the old characters and about all the mistakes Uncle Simon made when he first started farming. I know a lot more about the wild child you must have been too.' He grinned when she pulled a face at him.

The following morning they enjoyed their ride out on the horses, but Roseanne was careful not to accept any challenges that might involve forfeits. She was already more affected by Euan's company than she cared to admit. Afterwards, she cooked them both a good breakfast while Euan groomed and fed the horses, but she was anxious to be on her way, and wondering at herself for being so easily persuaded to change her plans.

The roads were quiet early on a Sunday morning and they chatted companionably.

'I suppose the new computers you've installed will be quite expensive?' she asked. 'What sort of arrangement did you come to with your uncle?'

'We didn't have time to go into details. Don't worry about it. It's not your problem. I have to stand much bigger outlays than this until a contract is complete. I expect Uncle K will sanction payment when he returns.'

Roseanne frowned. It was all she could do to refrain from telling him it was very much her concern. They never made changes without discussing them first and they always agreed a firm price in writing with the firm concerned before the work commenced. Simon Kershaw left the cash flow and costs entirely in her hands. Buying the meat and managing the processing plants were where his real interest and talents lay. Together they had made a good team, and Kershaw & Co. had expanded considerably.

'Do you have the key to your new flat yet?' Euan asked, interrupting her thoughts.

'Yes. Why?'

'We could pack some of the boxes straight into the van today and take them to the new place. There will be less to move next weekend.'

'You're determined to get me down to Ashburn next week aren't you?'

'If it's at all possible.' He grinned unrepentantly.

'I've been thinking about it anyway. I feel uneasy about the Lennoxes being away when the thieves could still be around. They'll notice there's no smoke from the chimneys in either the Lennoxes' house or the farmhouse, and no lights either if they're keeping watch. Some of the rare breed animals are kept specifically for breeding. They're almost irreplaceable. Any vehicle entering Ashburn has to drive past the Lennoxes' house. If they see it is empty the thieves might risk going into the farm yard instead of having to round up animals in a field. They would be easy to load from the sheds.'

Euan nodded his understanding. 'I hadn't thought of that, but I see what you mean,' he said slowly, ruefully accepting that if she did change her mind about next weekend it would be for the sake of the animals, not because she felt an irresistible attraction for him.

'Is there anything we can do about it?'

'Yes. I've been thinking I'll phone William and ask him to fix up some sort of time switch to have lights coming on in the hall at Ashburn, and maybe one of the bedrooms. I might telephone the local police and tell them the Lennoxes are away. They'll be more likely to check.'

'That's a good idea. And next weekend?'

'Mmm. I expect the police will be busy enough at the weekends so I ought to go down, but I need to hand over my keys to the new owners of my flat by five o'clock next Saturday. If you really do intend to help we could get most of my stuff to the new flat before then.' She grimaced. 'You'll have to excuse me if I turn up for work looking creased and crumpled next week.'

'I can't imagine that happening to our efficient Miss Fairfax. We'll move your clothes last thing and hang them straight into your new wardrobes.'

'Thank you. I shall be grateful for that.'

'There'll be a price to pay of course,' he said with a glint in his eyes.

'I thought there might be,' she replied dryly, 'but it will have to be a price I'm willing to pay.'

He wanted to say, 'I want to see a whole lot more of the real Roseanne. I want to spend both days and nights in your company.' Even as he thought these things he was amazed at himself. He had never had the slightest wish to get seriously involved with another human being. It had been a big enough commitment when his company had expanded so much he had needed to take on a partner, and even then he had not felt able to trust one man; instead, he had chosen two of his most reliable men and offered each of them a small percentage of his firm as working partners.

Instead, he said, 'I'd like you to show me round this area, and spend some time looking around Edinburgh.

Mother talked about going to North Berwick when she was young. Could we do that? Anything extra will be a bonus,' he added with another of those wicked grins.

'The most you'll get for a bonus will be a home-cooked dinner once I'm settled in,' Rosanne said darkly, 'so don't get your hopes up.'

'I shall look forward to that and be thankful for small mercies,' he said, with a smile which made Roseanne's heart give an unfamiliar lurch. She wished her insides wouldn't quiver every time he threw her one of those challenging looks.

7

They worked hard at the packing. Euan volunteered to deal with the kitchen and her bookshelves. He was surprisingly methodical and careful and Roseanne was amazed by the number of boxes they had had moved to her new flat by Sunday evening.

'You've been a tremendous help, Euan. I never thought we'd get so much done today. Do you fancy a Chinese takeaway?'

'That would be good. I'll get us a bottle of wine. If we relax for an hour we could finish packing anything else you'll not be needing during this next week.'

They sat in the remaining two armchairs with a tray each and the coffee table for their wine glasses.

'Here's to a long and happy future for both of us,' Euan said, clinking his glass to hers.

'I'm too tired to do any more packing tonight,' Roseanne said, stifling a yawn.

'How are you meaning to move these big chairs and your bed and dressing table without help?' Euan asked, assessing what was left.

'I'll ask Sam to give me a lift.'

'I suggest we move the rest of the boxes on Thursday evening after work and I'll help you with the big stuff on Friday afternoon. There's probably more here than we realise. We shall need a few more journeys yet.'

'Yes, sir. Thank you, sir,' Roseanne said with false meekness, reminding him she did not appreciate being organised.

He couldn't help himself though. It was his nature and one of the reasons he had made a success of his business, but more importantly he wanted to be sure of being able to spend next weekend with her at Ashburn. He got to his feet and stood looking down at her. 'I'll give you a pull up. You're obviously ready for bed when you're too tired to argue with me.' His eyes twinkled.

'For once I agree with you.'

He pulled her to her feet and right into his arms. He brushed her mouth gently but firmly with his lips, teasing hers open and giving a gentle nibble at her lower lip before he released her.

'Good night and sweet dreams,' he said softly, and let himself out.

* * *

'You're looking as fresh as new paint this morning, Roseanne, in spite of your busy weekend,' Euan greeted her. He was coming into the building as she was going across to the packing house to ask Eileen to save her more boxes.

'You scrub up well yourself. It's surprising what sleep and a shower can do.'

'Mmm. It would have been even better if we could have done that together too,' he said with a wicked grin as he went on his way.

During the morning Roseanne sent

an email to Mr K's laptop, telling him about the visit to Mr Arnold and the cattle rustlers, reporting on her telephone call to the police and her instructions to William about lights. She was astonished when she received a reply just before she switched off for the day.

'Dear Roseanne, thank you for keeping me informed. You've done all you can, especially alerting the police. We'll pray the thieves leave Ashburn alone. It didn't occur to me that Euan would be interested in visiting the farm. I am pleasantly surprised. It was good of you to take him with you and show him round. I thought you were planning to do your packing at the weekend ready for your move.'

Roseanne sat staring at the screen and reading the email again. He couldn't have forgotten he had asked her to show Euan around, could he? No, Mr K had an excellent memory. Something didn't quite add up. She had things to do so she switched off the computer and put it out of her mind — for now.

The processing lines were all running at full strength, which meant Roseanne and the rest of the office staff were kept busy too. Euan was spending most of his time watching how things were handled and getting to know the staff, assessing which ones would be capable of operating more modern machinery and who could be trained.

It had to be when they were all working flat out that one of the machines broke down. The firm who had installed them was very good with their back up service, not least because Kershaw & Co. paid their bills promptly, and expected prompt attention in return. The young service engineer arrived soon after lunch on Tuesday. He was alone this time, but the last time Roseanne had seen him he had been with the boss and still finishing his training. The workers urged him to get the repair done as fast as he could.

'This is putting us behind with an order for one of the big London stores,' the foreman told him anxiously. 'We can't afford to lose their trade.'

'I'm doing my best,' the young man said desperately, 'but this spare part I've brought doesnae seem to fit. The boss was certain it would be the right one.'

When Euan came striding across the yard, one of the women whispered, 'This is Mr K's nephew coming to see what's holding us up. He's a whizz with machines, they say.' Her words only made the young engineer more agitated. Euan's presence made him feel his fingers were all thumbs.

Euan watched a while but he couldn't keep silent any longer.

'Anyone can see that part is never going to fit in with the cog it is supposed to drive,' he said abruptly. Roseanne arrived in time to hear his critical tone.

'I'm sure your presence is only making Trevor more nervous, Euan.

This is the first time he has been here alone.'

'That may be so, but any fool can see that's not the right part, and the longer the machine is stopped the further behind we're getting with the order. It was supposed to be despatched tonight, I believe?'

'It was, but that's not Trevor's fault.'

The young man looked at her gratefully. 'He's right though, Miss Fairfax. It is the wrong part. Even worse, the works will be closed by the time I get back to pick up the right one.' He gave Roseanne a pleading glance. 'Could you phone and explain so that my boss gets all his bawling and growling over before I see him? A-and could you ask him if Jimmy could drop off the correct part at my mother's? Then I could leave at the crack of dawn tomorrow and get here early.'

'Very well, I'll do that,' Roseanne said, nodding resignedly. She turned to the rest of the group. 'The rest of you may as well go home early. We shall have to put in a long day tomorrow to catch up and get the order despatched as soon as we can.'

Roseanne arrived early the following morning but Trevor was already working at the plant and Euan was working with him, wearing his faded jeans and with his sleeves rolled up. Roseanne felt her stomach muscles clench. She couldn't understand why Euan should have such an effect on her. He looked up and caught her glance and grinned, almost as though he could read her thoughts. Roseanne blushed, then felt furious with herself. The two men seemed to be getting on all right and she left them to it to get her own work forward. She knew they would have to work late this evening if they were to make up time with the order. She had telephoned to explain the delivery would be delayed and had received a very brusque and chilly response from the man at the other end. They couldn't afford to lose such an important customer, especially during Mr K's absence.

It was almost midday before the machine was repaired, checked, cleaned and sterilised, ready to run. Roseanne knew all the workers and their circumstances, and she went across to the factory line to speak to Anne Gray. The young woman looked strained and tired.

'You can leave at your usual time this afternoon, Anne. I will take your place on the line myself.' She smiled. 'It will be good for me to keep in practice,' she assured her, and was rewarded by the gratitude on the young woman's face. Anne had ten-month-old twins and her husband worked shifts. His mother usually helped look after the children but she had not been in good health herself recently.

Euan was surprised when he saw Roseanne putting on a white coat and one of the hats worn by all the women on the processing line. It was almost the end of the day and the staff from the other plants were already leaving.

'Whatever are you doing?' he asked. She explained about Anne Gray.

'She is a good worker and she has been with us since she left school. Anyway, it will be good for me to keep myself trained up in the process and I would not have gone home until I knew the order was safely into the chilled lorry and on its way.'

'I see,' Euan said in bemused tones as he watched her tuck a few strands of her vibrant hair beneath the cap. 'What time do you expect to finish?'

'We should be loaded by about eight-thirty to nine o'clock I think, so it's not too late. I am glad Trevor made an effort to get here so early this morning though, or we would have been here until midnight.'

'Even so, you'll be hungry and tired. I tell you what, I'll cook dinner for both of us in the flat. Will you promise to come up as soon as you finish?'

'So long as you're not cooking steak pie or sausages! I couldn't face them tonight, however good they are.'

'All right, I promise to cook something light. I'm enjoying having a kitchen and doing some experimental cooking. Do you like fish?'

'Yes, but a salad would do. It is all I'd have the energy to make by the time I got home anyway.'

'I'll see what I can do to please your ladyship,' he said with a grin. Roseanne had to admit she enjoyed the pleasant camaraderie they had shared since the weekend they had spent at Ashburn. She frowned, recalling his uncle's strange comment regarding their visit to the farm. She must remember to ask Euan about that.

It had been a long day by the time everything was finished and made ready for the processing plant to begin all over again the following day. Although Roseanne was tired and almost wished she had said she would go straight home, she felt a glow of satisfaction at a job well done.

She climbed slowly up the steps to Mr K's flat. She had often been in it, so she knew it was spacious and surprisingly luxurious for a man of Uncle Simon's simple tastes.

'Ah, Roseanne, you look all in,' Euan greeted her warmly. 'I've put some towels to warm in the bathroom. I thought you might be glad of a shower to freshen up before we eat.'

'Oh I would, if the meal will wait. Something smells delicious.'

'You'll have to wait and see, but I'll pour you a glass of wine to take with you if you like. Red or white?'

'White please, with a large dash of soda water if you have any. Remember I have to drive home yet.'

'You don't have to. There's plenty of room here.' She looked at him sharply and saw that he was smiling but his eyes were serious and her heart thudded at the invitation in them. It would be all too easy to fall in with Euan Kennedy's wishes, and she suspected he was a man who was used to getting his own way.

Apart from the two large fluffy towels, there was an assortment of feminine toiletries to choose from. Euan's own shower gel and aftershave and toothpaste were set apart on a glass shelf. She wondered if he entertained other women while he had the whole place to himself in the evenings. Some of the workers started early and she was sure there would be some gossip before long if he did. The thought did not please her, yet she had no claim on him, she reminded herself.

Roseanne wished she had brought a change of clothes but she had not anticipated the day ending like this. At least she felt refreshed and clean and she had even tried the shampoo. She rubbed her hair vigorously, but it was long and thick and she had to leave it loose to dry. It was already curling around her face in damp tendrils when she returned to the living room.

'Oh, it is every bit as delightful as I imagined,' Euan exclaimed as soon as he saw her, and there was no denying the admiration in his eyes.

'What do you mean?'

'Your hair — hanging loose like that all around your shoulders. It looks more golden in the lamplight. It's beautiful.' He wondered what she would say if he drew her close and buried his face in the sweet-smelling tresses.

'I thought I would make use of the toiletries. Do you always keep a supply for the use of your lady friends?' She knew her voice was sharper than she had intended.

'Would you be a teeny bit jealous if I did?' he teased.

'Of course not. What you do in your leisure time is not my concern.'

'As a matter of fact I made a quick trip into the supermarket and brought the best they had on offer. I hope they were satisfactory?'

'They were.' She smiled now. 'More than satisfactory. Thank you for taking so much trouble.'

'I wanted some fresh salmon for our meal. I've made a salmon mousse so I hope it will have set in time. I've never used gelatine before and it took a bit longer than I expected.' He looked as anxious as a small boy.

'I'm sure it will be fine, Euan, but you should not have gone to all this trouble.'

'I aim to please, and I didn't want you having nightmares after a heavy and indigestible meal. Anyway, we have chilled melon cocktail for starters, so come and sit at the table while I bring it from the fridge.'

'Mmm, that was delicious,' Roseanne said as she cleared the last drop of juice from her dish. 'What's in it besides the melon?'

'The juice of an orange and a lemon, plus a light sugar syrup.'

'And? I'm sure I tasted something else, something different?'

'Oh maybe a wee touch of juice from the maraschino cherries, nothing much.'

'You're very modest. It was super, whatever your secret ingredient.'

'Can I pour you some wine?'

'Er, no thanks, better not risk it. It

wouldn't do if I was breathalysed on the drive home.'

'As I said, you can easily stay the night.'

'I think not, thank you. Can you imagine the gossip zinging around all the workshops by evening? Somebody would be sure to see me leaving in the morning. Anyway, I need a change of clothes.'

'Is it only the possibility of gossip which prevents you staying, Roseanne?' Euan's voice was serious now and his gaze was intense as he watched her. 'I would really like you to stay,' he added a little huskily.

'No, it's not the gossip, although I wouldn't like that either. I'm just not the type to sleep around.'

'I see.' Euan's mouth tightened. 'And I imagine there is the other small matter? The person you're moving in with? Mind you, you're not married, or even engaged.'

'What are you talking about?' Rose-anne asked, frowning slightly, brows raised in surprise.

'This Rob of yours, of course.'

'Rob?' Roseanne almost choked. 'I-I . . . ' She almost told him Rob would be delighted to think she had found a man who could tempt her from her virginal existence. 'I make my own decisions. If I was sure I really wanted to stay the night here, with you, then I would do so, whatever anyone else thought.'

'I see. Then it must be me. I don't measure up in some way. I shall have to try harder.'

'You certainly measure up as a cook. This salmon mousse and the salad are wonderful, so delicate, yet so tasty. I thought you said you never had the opportunity to do much cooking.'

'Don't change the subject, Rose-anne.'

'I'm not. Honestly, how did you know what to do?'

'My mother often made the melon and I remember helping her when I was a boy. I got the salmon recipe off the internet. I'm afraid the dessert is a meringue roulade, courtesy of the supermarket freezer,' he added with a grin.

'Oh my, you are spoiling me.' Rosanne grinned. Euan looked at her. She was not wearing a vestige of make-up and he wondered if she had any idea how lovely she was, how desirable.

'I've put the coffee on. You go through to the lounge and I'll bring it in.'

'I'll help you clear away and wash up first.'

'I'm a tidy worker. I clear as I go and the dishes will go in the dishwasher. I'm glad Uncle Simon likes his mod cons. I was rather surprised, actually, from the little I saw of him when we met.'

'I know,' Roseanne laughed. 'I don't think he would have thought of any of this himself. He had an up-and-coming young architect to design and oversee everything.'

Euan carried the tray of coffee

through and sat it on a low table with a small dish of chocolate mint wafers. Roseanne stifled a yawn, almost wishing she didn't need to drive home. At least the roads would be quiet at this time of night. As she sipped her coffee she could feel the tension rising between them and she knew Euan would try again to persuade her to stay. Her weakness astonished her. She couldn't deny he held a powerful attraction for her. She had never felt like this with any man before, and in so short a time too. She must be crazy. How Rob would smile if she ever found out.

So as soon as she had finished her coffee she put the cup back on the tray and stood up.

'Oh Roseanne, surely you don't need to leave so soon?' There was no mistaking the disappointment in Euan's eyes as he stood up too, bringing them close. He put his hands on her waist. 'Are you sure you wouldn't like to stay the night? I promise to let you sleep alone in the spare bedroom.'

'Better not,' she said half-heartedly. 'I don't want to start any gossip. Anyway, I do have a busy day tomorrow if I'm to move my boxes in the evening and get things forward for the weekend, remember. I must vacate my flat and hand in the keys before I go down to Ashburn.'

'I suppose you're right,' Euan said with a sigh, but instead of letting her go he slid his arms around her, drawing her against him, and his mouth sought hers. Euan's exploring fingers found the cool, bare skin beneath her shirt. His hand moved to discover the swell of her breasts and she gasped at his touch. Her stomach muscles clenched. He groaned softly and deepened his kisses. He was breathing hard. He raised his head.

'You're a very desirable woman, Roseanne,' he said huskily, and kissed her again, a long lingering kiss which left her breathless and weak with desire. 'I believe you want me almost as much as I want you,' he breathed softly. 'Please stay?'

'N-no.' Her breath was coming in little gasps and she was torn between an overwhelming desire for fulfilment and her innate caution. 'No, I mustn't stay. I can't. It's too soon.' She drew away. His arms fell to his sides. She picked up her handbag and made for the door. He went with her.

'Drive carefully, Roseanne.'

*   *   *

Afterwards, she wondered if it would have been better if she had stayed. Or would they have quarrelled anyway? Yes, she decided they would have disagreed, because Euan had made it clear he did not trust her. She shuddered. Trust was everything to her. How much worse it would have been if she had already given herself to him with all her heart and soul? For Roseanne knew there were no half measures for her. She would have been filled with bitter regret far worse than the emptiness she felt now . . .

8

Roseanne was surprised to see Euan already in his office when she arrived for work the following morning. She surmised that he had wanted to get his work forward so that he would be free to help her move and she smiled inwardly and felt a glow of warmth. She could not know he had been too wide awake and frustrated to sleep after she had left him the previous evening. She had been deadly tired herself after the hectic day, but she had not slept well and she had come to work early too.

When she looked more closely, she thought Euan looked as though he had been at his desk half the night. Surely there couldn't be a fault with the new computer system, she thought with a silent groan. His jacket was draped around a chair back and his hair looked tousled as though he had tugged his fingers through it several times. He was staring at something on the main computer, and judging by his expression whatever he saw did not please him.

Her own thoughts moved to the day ahead. She wanted to do some shopping to stock the fridge and shelves in her new flat, as well as move her boxes. She had received a postcard from Robinia to say that things were going splendidly and she expected to finish her current assignment a week earlier than planned.

'It will take me several days to move my things from Mother's. After that we'll have fun giving your lovely hunk of beef a good roasting.'

Roseanne was not so keen to play tricks or deceive Euan since they had spent more time together. She wished she had never mentioned him to Robinia. She was no longer sure she wanted to introduce him to her vivacious sister at all. Would he kiss Rob as he had kissed her? Of course he would, if he got the chance. Would her sister go all the way and sleep with him? Or did she exaggerate her escapades to shock Roseanne because she was the elder, more serious sister? Rob had always been a tease, but there had never been any jealousy between them, so why did Roseanne's cheeks feel hot as she pictured Rob and Euan together? She couldn't deny a twinge of envy when she considered how easily Robinia had men falling over themselves to do her bidding with no more than a flicker of her long, dark lashes. It had never mattered before, but she had never been attracted to any of the men they both knew.

Euan looked up when he heard her opening the door to her office. His face looked grim and his eyes seemed strained as though he had been staring at the computer for hours. Roseanne knew he kept in touch with his own business by telephone and computer, but he had his own up-to-the-minute machine for that in the flat, and right now he was apparently working on the new computer he had installed in his uncle's office.

In fact, Euan had found it impossible to sleep after Roseanne had left the previous evening. She disturbed him more than any woman he had ever met. After a few hours of tossing and turning he had showered and dressed and come into the office, determined to make one more comprehensive check on the new system in the offices before he turned his attention to the processing and packaging machines.

'Is there a problem with the new system?' she called cheerfully through his open door.

'You might consider it's working too well,' he said abruptly. 'Come in here and close the door. It's time we had a serious talk, Miss Fairfax.' It was not only his formal address which sent shivers down Roseanne's spine, it was his expression of chilling contempt. Yet there was a strange look in his grey eyes — not hurt exactly. Disillusionment?

Disappointment, perhaps? Had the new system not come up to his expectations? She frowned. She didn't like his stern expression. She went into his office and closed the door.

'What's the trouble?'

'You are.'

'I am?' Roseanne was genuinely surprised.

'I suppose you think you can fool my uncle, a middle-aged man with no university education, and apparently no family to look out for him, to check up on you, or interfere?' Roseanne stiffened, staring at him, but she remained silent, waiting. She took a deep breath, struggling to control her emotions. She had learned it was always better to wait for the whole picture, but she was chilled by his scathing tone. This Euan Kennedy was a ruthless stranger; a cold, hard man.

'Well?' he snapped. 'I suppose my uncle leaves all the accounts to you because you have a degree in accountancy?'

'He leaves all the accounts to me because he knows I'm capable of doing them. He trusts me, as I trust him with his side of the business — the buying and processing. We share the marketing side of our products.'

'Oh yes, I can believe he trusts you,' he sneered. 'More fool him! You almost had me fooled too.'

Roseanne could feel her temper rising but she drew herself up tall and straight. 'Whatever you have to say, get on with it,' she said coldly, as though he was a stammering schoolboy. Euan's grey eyes flashed at her cool tone. His own staff respected him, every last one of them. They knew he worked as hard as any of them and that he was fair and honest and expected the same in return.

'I'm not an accountant, but I've run my own business long enough to understand accounts. I've met people I can trust and some who think they are smart, people like you who can't be trusted with someone else's money.'

Roseanne gasped, but he went on coldly, 'I considered myself a good judge of character. It's one of the reasons I've made a success of my own business. But I also keep my finger on the pulse and I check on every detail.'

'I believe Kershaw & Co. is a success for the same reason. We also keep a close eye on the details.'

'We!' he bellowed. 'There you go again, the royal 'we'. Who the devil do you think you are? You're my uncle's employee and you're robbing him blind.' He felt a pang of compunction for his brutal words when he saw her flinch. He watched the colour drain from her cheeks. In his heart he knew he was more furious because he had been completely taken in by her than because she was using the firm's money for her personal benefit.

'You're making a very serious accusation,' Roseanne stated in the steeliest voice she could muster. 'For your own sake I hope you have proof for whatever you're implying.' Her cool tone, her apparent composure, made Euan's blood boil.

'Of course I have proof,' he said. 'I told you I could access everything from any of the computers on this central one.'

'So? I believe everything is in order and up to date.'

'Oh yes, it is up to date. Right to the latest bank statement.'

'You have the passwords? You can access the bank accounts?' Roseanne's eyes widened. She hadn't thought that could be possible. She had been working on the latest reconciliation yesterday afternoon before she left the office to take her place on the production line. 'Only Mr Kershaw and myself know the passwords.'

'I have the firm's bank reconciliation up on my screen now, checked and reconciled by yourself.'

'Does your uncle know you have access to all the firm's affairs?' Roseanne asked coldly.

'Probably not. I got the impression

he has not kept abreast with modern developments, which, my dear Miss Fairfax, is one of the reasons you knew you had free rein to do exactly as you pleased. No doubt he also leaves the banking to you too.'

'Of course he does; it's part of my job. But it is none of your business what we do, or how we do it. If you were checking to see whether we can pay you your money, then I can assure you we always pay our debts. But you may not even be who you say you are, for all I know. Even if you are Simon Kershaw's nephew, you are a stranger to him.'

'I have been a stranger to him until now, but it is obvious you are taking advantage of your position, believing he has no one of his own. Clearly it's time he had someone to protect his interests.'

Roseanne bit hard on her lower lip in an effort to control her temper and hide her hurt at his mistrust. His words had the painful thrust of a knife through her heart. 'Your uncle may look like every child's picture of a cherubic Santa Claus, but appearances are deceptive. No one — but no one — would get away with cheating him, certainly not a second time. He may not like computers, but he frequently takes home printouts of balance sheets and bank statements, and he studies them carefully, especially when we're considering changes. He has an excellent memory for figures, but he relies on me to keep him up to date with cash flow. That is my job, and it's in the interests of everyone at Kershaw's that I should do it well.'

'It seems to me there are several things in your interests — personal interests.'

'That is the second time you've made veiled accusations. If you have something to say, then say it,' she snapped. 'Otherwise keep your opinions to yourself.'

'Come round here and see the figures. They're substantial sums for a mere employee to be squirreling away.'

Although her conscience was clear, Roseanne found her heart thumping as she moved round the desk to view the computer screen. She was hurt that Euan mistrusted her. She wished she didn't care what he thought. She had never cheated in her life.

She slipped into his seat as he moved aside but she was tense, her back ramrod straight. Grimly he bent over her, intensely aware of the fresh citrus scent of her hair. He moved the mouse until he had highlighted the two amounts which caused him to doubt her integrity. Roseanne sensed the implacable steel of a businessman who was used to being right. In his own business he called the tune. Her resolve hardened but she felt trapped between him and the desk.

'Explain these — if you can,' he snapped. She stared at the screen.

'Ah . . . ' she breathed. She could understand why he might be suspicious, but surely he could have trusted her, or at least asked for an explanation? How could he believe she would cheat a man she had known all her life, a man she regarded with affection and respect? She was tempted to tell him she was a partner in the firm, but if his uncle had wanted him to know surely he would have told him?

'I think you had better ask your uncle for an explanation.'

'You mean he knows?' He stared at her in disbelief.

'Of course he knows,' Roseanne snapped, angered by his scepticism. 'Anyone *who matters* knows,' she added sarcastically. She would have stood to face him but he was too close. 'I resent you prying into my personal affairs.'

'I'll bet you do,' he sneered, 'but be assured I shall call your bluff. If you can offer an explanation for what amounts to fraud, or at least embezzlement . . . ' Roseanne gasped at that, but he ignored her and went on coldly, 'Then you had better explain now, because make no mistake I shall ask my uncle when he returns. I have no desire to spoil his holiday by tackling this immediately, but I don't intend to stand aside and let you take advantage of an old man. I imagine you thought you could do what you liked when he had no one else to look out for him.'

'I look out for him,' she said coldly, 'as he has looked out for me since my grandfather died, and even before then.'

'Answer me this then — why are all the rest of the staff in the firm's pension scheme while you have a personal pension paid for by the company?'

'I would answer if it was any of your business,' Roseanne said coldly. 'It was set up at your uncle's instigation. I agreed because it was good advice.'

'I'll bet you did,' he snapped, wishing he didn't feel so disillusioned. 'What about the life insurance? Why should the company pay for that? It is no benefit to anyone except you.'

'Maybe, maybe not. As I said, you must ask your uncle.'

'But it's dishonest! You're paying

your own insurance out of the firm's money.'

'Take it up with your uncle — if you're arrogant enough to believe this is any of your concern. Since you seem to have set yourself up as a personal investigator, it's a pity you didn't postpone your visit until Mr Kershaw was here in person to answer your questions.'

She stood up quickly, taking him by surprise. He was even closer than she had realised, but she'd had enough. Inwardly she was trembling, but she stepped away and faced him, willing herself to stay calm.

'I think he would resent your interference as much as I do. He's not an old man. He's considerably younger than your mother, I believe, and he's certainly not senile. He'll probably still have his finger on the pulse of this company thirty years from now when he's eighty.'

She put her hand flat against his chest to push him away but he stood rock-solid.

'I have work to do,' she said icily. The office was soundproof, but two sides of it were glass and the rest of the staff were at their desks now. They would all realise she was furious by the flags of colour on her cheekbones and the way her eyes blazed. She marched to the door, but before she opened it she swung round to face him again.

'While we're talking about cheating and deceit, I'd advise you not to judge everybody by your own standards. You owe me an explanation and an apology.'

'An apology? I don't think so,' Euan snapped sharply, wondering why he felt he had fought a battle and lost a war.

'Your uncle knew nothing about the email instructing me to take you down to Ashburn. You manipulated me, as well as your mother. Don't speak to me again until you have an explanation.' She turned and walked briskly to her own office, leaving his door wide open, as it had been when she arrived. She knew now he had been waiting for her.

She was filled with anger and

disappointment, and most of all she was hurt. Surely she had just as much reason to distrust him, coming into the offices and taking over his uncle's place, sifting through the accounts on the pretext of checking the workings of the new computer system. It was fortunate that he had only discovered access to the day-to-day accounts and not the company's balance sheet and capital accounts. Supposing he was an impostor? She stood still as a statue for a second. But no . . . She flopped into her chair, her elbows on the desk as she stared into space. No, he was no impostor. He and Mr K had met at the airport and Mr K had phoned to tell her of his arrival — to *warn* her of his arrival. She frowned. Why did he think she needed warning? What exactly had he said in that brief phone call? His nephew would be arriving. He would be reviewing the company's office computers. 'He will probably install new ones — but don't let him persuade you to do anything you don't want to do, lassie.'

She frowned. What had Mr K had in mind? He'd told her his nephew had a forceful personality. 'He's needed it to get where he is today,' he'd added, 'but you and I will decide what's best for Kershaw & Co.'

He'd rung off in a hurry to catch his plane. She'd had no opportunity to ask questions. In her mind she went over their brief conversation. She always tried to see all sides of any dispute and assess situations fairly. It was one of the reasons the workers came to her if they had problems. Since Euan Kennedy could access so much about their business affairs, she could understand why he might wonder why her personal pension and insurance were paid through the firm. In her heart, she knew what had really upset and dismayed her was that Euan did not trust her. Why had he thought it necessary to check up at all? How could he make such assumptions without even consulting her or his uncle first?

It took her a long time to settle to her

work that morning and several times she made mistakes and had to re-check. Consequently she was not finished as early as she had intended. By the time she was ready to leave, Sam was waiting for her with the van at the front door, swinging the keys in his hand.

'Thanks, Sam. I'll leave my car here tonight. I'll bring the van back in the morning.'

'It was a good job you phoned through to tell me you wanted the keys tonight, Miss Roseanne. Mr Kennedy came down for the van half an hour ago but I told him I'd other instructions. He wasnae very pleased,' he added anxiously. 'I dinnae ken why he wanted it. I told him he could use it any night next week. He said that was no bloody good to him.'

'Don't worry, Sam. I'll sort out Mr Kennedy. He'd no right to speak to you like that.'

'Och, I dinnae mind,' he said with a grin, 'but I wouldn't like to cause any trouble with the boss's nephew. Now

183

you're sure you don't need a lift with all your boxes?'

'Not tonight, thanks, Sam. I could do with some help with some pieces of furniture tomorrow though, please.'

'I'll be ready, lassie. Good night and take care.'

9

Roseanne didn't stop to eat an evening meal. Her stomach had churned all day and she chided herself constantly for allowing Euan to get under her skin to such an extent, but she hated being misjudged. She hated quarrels too. She straightened her slim shoulders. Her conscience was clear. She would not be cowed by Euan Kennedy, however much he attracted her physically. She changed into an old T-shirt and a pair of scruffy jeans that seemed to have shrunk. She began carrying the boxes to the van. She had stowed away about half a dozen but when she arrived with her next precarious load, a tall figure was leaning against the van. He looked relaxed and at ease, and Roseanne's temper flared at the sight of that rueful smile lifting the corner of his well-shaped mouth. She noticed the quizzical look in his grey eyes. How dare he come here as though nothing had happened between them?

'What do you think you're doing?' she demanded, almost toppling the top box onto the ground. Euan caught it and placed it carefully in the van and turned to take the next one from her.

'I can manage perfectly well on my own,' she snapped. 'Go away.'

'I promised to help you move the remaining boxes.'

'And I told you not to speak to me until you'd apologised for your trickery.'

'We could work in silence, I suppose,' he suggested, raising one brow ironically. 'Or I can apologise for using a little subterfuge to get you down to Ashburn. I can't say I'm sorry, because I wanted your company, and if you're honest I think you enjoyed the weekend too — all of it.'

She glared at him and cursed at the way her colour rose. She knew he was remembering the forfeit he had claimed, or maybe the chocolate kisses.

His expression changed and he looked grave. 'As to the business this morning . . . ' He tried to take her arm but she shrugged him off. 'We need to talk, Roseanne, but not out here on the pavement. Can't we go inside?'

'Can't you see I'm busy? Anyway, we did more than enough talking this morning.'

'All right, I'll help you load up the rest of the boxes and then we'll have something to eat before we unload them. We can talk while we eat,' he said.

'And how would you know I want to eat, especially in your company? As for talking to you, I want that even less.' Roseanne stood with her hands on her slim hips and glared at him. She was not ready to forgive and forget, however much she might like to wipe out this morning's scene.

'You haven't had time to eat. I saw you leave in the van. I was going to bring it for you but Sam refused to let me have the keys. All the staff are very loyal to you. There's been a distinctly chilly air where ever I went today.'

Roseanne turned away to hide the glimmer of a smile which threatened to spoil her haughty and unforgiving stance. Her mother had always said she boiled up swiftly but cooled quickly too, but she didn't believe anything could dispel the hurt she felt at being so badly misjudged by Euan.

He ignored her silence and insisted on helping her load the rest of the boxes. Then he ran up the stairs two at a time while she locked the van doors. She was tempted to drive away and leave him, but the keys to her new home were still inside. Slowly she climbed the stairs. She'd only had a cup of coffee and half a sandwich at lunchtime and her stomach was beginning to make hollow rumbles. Euan had switched on the grill and a hot plate.

'Will bacon and eggs do? Your fridge is almost empty.'

'What else would you expect? I'm moving tomorrow,' she snapped. 'Anyway,

I've not invited anyone to supper, as far as I'm aware.'

He went on laying rashers of bacon and halved tomatoes on the grill pan, then set them to cook. He turned and reached for the only two glasses in the cupboard. 'A tumbler will have to do,' he said, pouring her some white wine.

'Don't pour that for me,' she snapped. 'I'm driving.'

'I'll drive the van. Drink up. It will relax you.'

'If you mean it will mellow me you'll be wrong. Too much wine can make me very argumentative.'

'All right.' He sighed heavily. 'Please yourself.'

She did. She drained the glass. It was not a good idea on an empty stomach. She hooked a foot round the remaining stool and drew it towards her, sitting down with a heavy sigh. She watched as he sliced bread. He had his back to her so she couldn't see his face.

'I telephoned Australia,' he said. 'I didn't want to interrupt Uncle Simon's

189

holiday but . . . ' He shrugged. 'I had to know why you were so furious. Why you looked so — so hurt. Mother said they were just about to eat their meal. Uncle Simon was decidedly sharp and irritable. I don't know whether it was because he was hungry or because I'd had the audacity to query anything concerning his perfect Miss Fairfax's administration.'

'In other words he gave you a flea in your ear,' Roseanne said bluntly. He glared at her. She couldn't prevent a splutter of laughter. 'It's the wine,' she choked. 'Shouldn't have had it on an empty stomach.'

'I see.' He frowned, only half-believing her. He broke the four remaining eggs into the frying pan. 'In that case you'd better eat and then we'll talk.'

'Nothing to talk about. You think I'm dishonest. I hate you for that. Why don't you go away and leave me in peace.'

'Here, eat this lot,' he said, placing a

plate of bacon and tomatoes in front of her then adding two fried eggs.

'I can't eat all that! I'm not a baby elephant.'

'Eat what you can, then.' He passed the crusty loaf she had bought at the bakery on the way home and she took a piece.

'You're not very good at slicing bread, are you?' she said, examining the wedge-shaped slice. He didn't answer and they ate in silence. Roseanne couldn't believe it when she'd cleared her plate. She hadn't realised she was so hungry. Euan poured two mugs of coffee. She sipped hers slowly, and the world didn't seem such a bad place after all. She looked across at Euan and saw that he seemed to be lost in his own thoughts. She cleared away the dishes and began to wash them. He dried them in silence.

'Whatever you have to say, for goodness sake get it over with,' she said impatiently. 'It can't be any worse than the things you said this morning.'

'I know. That's the trouble. I owe you a huge apology, and I'm not used to needing to apologise. I'm so used to making my own judgments and taking decisions. I find it difficult to accept things on trust.'

He looked her in the eye and the humility she saw there, which tugged her heart strings more than she cared to admit. But she remained silent, waiting.

'You're right,' Euan continued, 'Uncle Simon did tear a strip off me.' He grimaced. 'He made me feel like a little school boy. He didn't give me chance to say my concerns were purely for him, or even what I wanted to ask. He said so long as you were in charge he had no worries as far as Kershaw & Co. goes. At the airport he had asked a few questions about my own business strategy. He seemed to guess we might strike sparks off each other. He reminded me that he had warned me not to disagree with you about anything to do with Kershaw & Co.'

'Your uncle trusts me, as I trust him

— implicitly.' Roseanne nodded. 'I wouldn't have stayed with the company otherwise. He's the nearest person I've known to a father figure.'

'I think I can understand that,' Euan said carefully, 'but I still don't know why your personal finances have anything to do with the firm's accounts. All my instincts told me you were as honest and trustworthy as my Uncle said — which is more than I can say for many of the people I have known, especially given the wide scope of your responsibilities in the firm. I'm usually a fair judge of character, but you are different to anyone I've known. I suppose that's why I felt doubly angry and disillusioned when I stumbled across those figures. Surely you can admit they look as though you're feathering your nest at Uncle Simon's expense?'

'I suppose it might to someone who doesn't understand the way we work,' Roseanne admitted slowly.

'Are they in lieu of some kind of bonus?'

'I can see you still don't trust me,' Roseanne snapped.

'I suppose the payments could be in lieu of a bonus, or something. I hadn't thought of that.'

'Why don't you wait and discuss the matter in full with your uncle when you see him — if you really think it is any of your business.'

'You still haven't forgiven me, I can see that. I've hurt you . . . '

'Yes. I'm not used to anyone mistrusting me. That is hard to forgive, or forget.'

'Oh Roseanne, I can't tell you how sorry I am. And after hearing Uncle Simon on the other end of the telephone, I reckon he can take care of himself, and you. I got a distinct feeling he was protecting you in some way. But why should you need protecting, especially from me, his own nephew?'

'Why indeed,' Roseanne muttered. 'I suppose you may be his relative, but you must admit you're a stranger to him. He has known me all my life.

Maybe he needs time to get to know you.'

'He certainly didn't sound like a cuddlesome daddy, that's for sure.'

'He can be tough when he needs to be. Did he explain away your suspicions?' she asked coldly, grimly, still smarting from his opinion of her as a possible cheat, even though she could see why he might jump to such conclusions from the figures he had seen in the accounts.

'He didn't let me get round to the details. In any case I don't think Uncle Simon considered there was anything he needed to explain, at least not to me. All I got was a curt goodbye!'

'Good,' she said with satisfaction, her green eyes gleaming. He suspected she was holding back a smile. Was she laughing at his discomfort?

'I'm still furious with you for doubting my integrity. I can't forgive you for that.' She held up her hand to silence him. 'But I've had time to realise there are things you don't know about the company and the way we work. In the circumstances, perhaps I'd have reached the same conclusion. But I hope I'd have handled the situation more diplomatically until I knew all the circumstances.'

Euan felt like a school boy who'd had his knuckles wrapped. 'Fair enough,' he said. 'I really am sorry I've made an arse of things. Can we at least be friends?' He couldn't remember ever needing to plead with a woman before, but deep down he really wanted to be friends with Roseanne — more than friends. If his uncle could put so much trust in her, why shouldn't he?

'Perhaps if he'd known you well enough, or if you'd had more time together, your uncle would have explained more. As it is . . . ' She shrugged. 'You'll have to wait until he returns.'

Euan noticed she had not agreed to be friends and he felt more disappointed than he liked to admit. He'd been a fool to accuse her the way he had and he regretted it bitterly, but he had been tired and frustrated, then disappointed. He still had no proof his earlier suspicions were unfounded though, but he didn't believe anyone could look him straight in the eye, as Roseanne certainly did, if they were guilty of the smallest sin.

Roseanne was exhausted by the time she fell into bed, but she knew she would have been more exhausted without Euan's help. They had worked most of the time in silence. It was not the earlier, angry silence but it was unlikely they could return to the blossoming friendship they had shared during their weekend at Ashburn, and she regretted that.

* * *

Roseanne was relieved when William telephoned from Ashburn early on Friday morning.

'The police asked us to thank you for letting them know Mr and Mrs Lennox are away and that the farmhouse is empty. They have been really diligent,' he said.

'I'm glad to hear it,' Roseanne said, 'but has your grandfather noticed any suspicious characters lurking around?'

'He hasn't, but he thinks they would be more likely to creep about on foot during the night to discover the layout and where the animals are grazing.'

'Mmm, I expect he's right,' Roseanne agreed anxiously.

'One of the policemen used to live in the village when he was a boy and he remembers coming to see Mr Kershaw's rare breed animals. He reckons there will be a big outcry in the newspapers if some of them are stolen and killed for meat. They have given us a direct number to telephone to save time going through emergency services if we see anything suspicious. They asked if you and Mr Kershaw would agree to join the Farm Watch scheme. It is only getting going round here. They reckon it hasn't taken off in this area with local farmers because we haven't had any trouble until recently.'

'I didn't know there was a local Farm Watch scheme round Ashburn, but it sounds a good idea.'

'Aye, even Granddad agrees. Apparently they telephone alerts through to mobiles if there is anything suspicious in the area. A lot of quad bikes have gone missing in some places. The police are going to come and tell Mr Lennox more about it next week.'

'That's excellent, William,' Roseanne said with relief.

'Mmm, but they did say they are always busier at weekends with other trouble, so they can't guarantee as many patrols round our rural area.'

'That's fair enough. I'm hoping to be down there myself if all goes to plan. I hope to drive down on Saturday morning if I get all my stuff moved, and if I can leave my keys with the estate agent.'

Later in the day she told Euan about William's phone call.

'We'll both go down to Ashburn,' he said promptly. 'I'll collect you early. We should be there well before lunch.'

'There's no need. I'm used to driving down on my own. Anyway, your uncle seemed surprised that you wanted to see the farm. I still don't know how you manoeuvred that, by the way,' she added accusingly.

'Uncle Simon doesn't know what interests I have. I used to spend some of my holidays with a school friend who lived on a vast sheep farm in the outback. Anyway, I'd rather be there with you. Who knows what trouble there could be while Mr Lennox is away and with the farmhouse empty?'

Roseanne knew he was right, and she couldn't dispel an uneasy feeling herself about the thieves. It was unlikely they would only target one farm. She was ready and waiting on Saturday morning and they arrived at Ashburn before eleven.

'I suggest we call in at the post office,' Roseanne said. 'I'll get some fresh rolls and a newspaper.'

'And the shop keeper will advertise our presence at Ashburn,' Euan murmured with a knowing glint in his eye. 'See, I'm getting to know about the locals already.'

'Exactly. If Mrs Strang asks when we're going back I'll say you may be staying on, shall I?'

'All right.' Euan nodded. 'I was wondering how you feel about us staying until Monday morning. We could leave at six-thirty and be at Kershaw's before the office staff arrive.'

'We'll see,' she said. 'I suppose if thieves have been snooping around they'll expect the farmhouse to be deserted on Sunday evenings. I'm glad Mr and Mrs Lennox will be back before next weekend.'

'I'm not so sure I am.' Euan grinned. 'At least their absence has helped me persuade you to accompany me down here for one more weekend.'

★   ★   ★

Euan was surprised at the number of people who came to greet them when they arrived at the village hall for the concert that evening.

'This is where you really belong, isn't it? You're one of them, Roseanne.'

'I've been coming here all my life, but I see some of the women are wondering what your connection is,' she said with a nod towards three young women who were nudging each other and casting him admiring glances. He wanted to tell her there was only one woman in the room who interested him, even though he had probably blown his chances with her.

'Will they expect you to stay back stage?' he whispered.

'No. I shall only be on for a duet in each half of the concert to add a bit of variety and while some of them change costumes.'

The audience was obviously familiar with the ballad about the wee bawbee which the young man had left with his sweetheart when he left to seek his fortune years before. They almost raised the roof with claps and cheers when the couple were reunited with a kiss at the end. Euan felt it was a longer kiss than necessary, and he was dismayed at the pang of jealousy he felt towards the personable young man who was singing with Roseanne.

'Who is he?' he asked Jock McIntyre, who was sitting on his other side.

'He's the manager frae Laird Gallaby's estate. He's known Roseanne since they went to Sunday school. He was sweet on her until she and her sister played a trick on him. He didn't forgive either o' them for a long time. He thought they'd made a fool of him.' The old man chuckled. 'Mind you, he was making the most o' yon kiss tonight. He fairly brought the colour to Roseanne's cheeks. Did ye notice?'

'Yes, I did. Is he married?'

'He was. He's divorced now.' He eyed Euan speculatively. 'You ever been married?'

'No. I was never tempted to go that

far,' Euan said, shaking his head. He could have added 'until now'. Was he seriously so tempted by Roseanne, in spite of his misgivings over his uncle's accounts? Jock was nodding with satisfaction as Roseanne came back to her seat beside them.

'You have a good voice,' Euan said during the interval as they accepted the tea and biscuits which were being passed round. 'I like the richness of it. Is that what they call a mezzo soprano?'

'I wouldn't know.' Rosanne laughed. 'I've never been for singing lessons but I can hardly get out of it here.'

'They appreciate your talent.'

'I'm glad someone does,' she said dryly, and he knew she was remembering his accusations. He'd had plenty of time to reflect and he couldn't believe he'd blundered in like a blind ox with a loaded wagon, whatever the figures said.

As they drove home afterwards, Roseanne knew Euan was doing his best to make up for their earlier altercation. She understood the reason he had reached the conclusions but she couldn't forget the hurt she felt at his mistrust.

'I told William I would exercise the horses in the morning. I want to have a ride around the boundary fences to make sure there are no gaps and no reason for the animals to stray. No excuse for thieves to drive them away.'

'I'll come with you, if I may?' Euan suggested. Roseanne was surprised at him asking with such humility.

'If you wish. I'm having my breakfast first — about seven o'clock, then it doesn't matter if I take all morning. Would that suit you?'

'Sounds fine to me.' He held her elbow as they negotiated the rough path from the car to the house. He would have liked to kiss her goodnight but she had erected an invisible barrier since their quarrel and he had no idea how to breach it. At least she hadn't objected to him riding with her in the morning. He would have to be content to go back to square one and take one step at a time. He wondered why it mattered so much. He still didn't understand the entries he had queried in his uncle's business accounts, and she had not made any effort to explain, or even to excuse them, yet still every instinct told him Roseanne was not the type of woman who would cheat anyone, and certainly not a man she regarded as almost a father. There was no doubt she worked hard on behalf of the company too.

It was a bright, breezy morning, the sort of day Roseanne loved for riding. She made up her mind to forget Euan's opinion of her. What did it matter anyway? He would soon be going to Australia, and probably returning to America once he had visited his mother. She would probably never see him again. She would take a leaf out of Robinia's book. Her sister enjoyed each moment and moved on to the next — or so she had always said.

'All the fences are in excellent order,'

she said as they came to the last stretch which would bring them back to the farm yard. 'I expected they would be. Mr Lennox is very conscientious about such things. William told me the police discovered the thieves had cut the fence wires at Mr Arnold's so they could herd his sheep into a small enclosure near the loading pens.'

'Perhaps they've taken enough risks in this area and moved on somewhere else,' Euan suggested.

'I hope you're right, but if they know this area at all they're bound to know Ashburn has some of the best quality beef cattle. They would get a higher price for them.'

After they had groomed the horses and turned them out into the paddock, Euan suggested they should change and go to the village pub for their Sunday lunch. He was delighted when she agreed. They received several cheery greetings. Euan realised most of the locals seemed to know now that he was Simon Fairfax's nephew and therefore welcome in their small community. Much later, Roseanne was astonished when she looked at her watch and realised half the afternoon had flown away in friendly chatter.

'They're all so pleased to see you,' Euan said. 'It was hard to get away when they all wanted to chat.'

'I suspect most of them were more curious to find out about you. They all know me well enough.'

They walked in companionable silence as they made their way back to Ashburn, both of them enjoying the sunshine and fresh air, but not yet so at ease that Euan felt he could take her hand, or draw her closer as he longed to do.

'I'm going to get the records up to date and pay any bills which are due,' Roseanne said as they reached the house.

'I'd like to see your farm computer programmes sometime,' Euan said. He saw Roseanne's quick frown. He stopped and turned to face her. 'I wish I'd never seen those bloody bank statements for Kershaw & Co. and I wish I didn't have such a nose for sniffing things out. You have my word I shall not try to interfere with anything else, even if I knew anything about animal records — which I don't. I'm simply interested in all things to do with computers. I've learned more since I set up in business than I ever did at university.'

'Yes, I suppose I could say the same. Grandfather always said it was a day wasted when you didn't learn something new, so I expect we all go on learning. I'll show you the farm computers if we're both down here together again. I'm for an early night tonight, though, if we're to get away at the crack of dawn and be back before anyone arrives at the offices. I have a lot of sorting out of my own to do at the flat this week too.'

Euan wondered if she was giving him a hint to keep his distance, but her expression showed no anger or resentment now.

* ★ ★

Roseanne didn't know what had wakened her. She lay on her back in the dark, listening intently. Her part of the house had been modernised to her own taste and her bedroom was the largest and the only one with windows looking to both back and front. A beam of light swept briefly across her ceiling. It came from the yard side. The green light from her digital alarm clock was sufficient to let her grope her way to the window. She caught her breath when she glimpsed what seemed to be the rear lights of a vehicle. She hadn't seriously believed thieves would risk striking again so close to Mr Arnold's, but as she watched she realised there was a vehicle and a trailer and it was turning into the old part of the farm steading where the pigs were housed. Whoever it was must have managed to open the bottom gates into the farm as well as negotiating the narrow entrance into the old farm steading. Maybe that was what had wakened her, the sweep of lights through her bedroom window. There were gates to the old steading too, but they were rarely needed these days. They were very long, made of iron, and very heavy. She and Euan had considered closing them as an extra precaution before they went to bed, then changed their minds when they saw the stiff, rusty hinges. Swiftly she pulled on her jeans and a sweater, thrusting her feet into sandals as she ran to Euan's room. She didn't wait for an answer to her knock before she opened the door.

'Don't put on your light!' she hissed softly. 'We've got intruders. They're heading into the old farm steading. They must have managed to open the bottom gates without disturbing the McIntyres. I'm going to shut the top gates to delay their escape.'

'No! Wait for me. There may be several of them. They could be dangerous.'

'There's no time to wait!'

'Then you shut the bottom gates below the milking parlour. I'll deal with the top ones. That will make doubly sure of holding them back. Jock McIntyre was convinced they'd make a try.'

'All right,' Roseanne agreed, hastily backing out of the room, aware of his muscular torso and the long bare legs already kicking off the duvet. 'I'll phone the McIntyres from my mobile. They'll alert the police,' she called back softly as she ran down the stairs.

They both moved swiftly and silently but it was some distance to the lower gates leading onto the road beside the McIntyres' cottage. Roseanne had the McIntyres' number in her memory list. She phoned as she ran. Mrs McIntyre answered on the second ring.

'It's me, Roseanne. We've got trouble.'

'I'll phone the police.

'We're shutting the gates,' Roseanne panted, glad Mrs McIntyre was not a woman who panicked or asked questions. Roseanne knew she could rely on her. The McIntyres had obviously been prepared and half expecting the thieves would try for Ashburn stock.

She had just swung the gates shut and was fixing the bolts when William came running, still pulling on his sweater. 'We've been bringing the tractor down to our cottage at nights in case we needed it for a barricade. Did you manage to shut the top gates? They're very wide. It makes them heavy, especially if you're in a hurry.'

'Euan is shutting them now. The thieves have driven right into the old farm steading so they must have expected the house to be empty. If Euan manages to shut the gates, that should be enough to hold them until the police get here.'

'Yes, I'll . . . Ah, here's Granddad with the tractor as a backup. We'll not let the devils get away with our animals.'

Euan was less familiar with the layout in the dark. One of the top gates was folded back against the wall and he released the catch and swung it into place fairly easily, but the other gate was longer, with a triangular support on the top for extra strength to try and prevent it from sagging, but that made it heavier. It was hinged to the shed so that it could be swung two ways for guiding the animals, but it was rarely needed these days and the hinges were stiff, making it more difficult to swing. Euan knew the thieves were already shifting animals by the squealing of the pigs and the cursing and hissing of one of the men. As he tugged at the heavy gate one end dragged on the concrete. It made a loud scraping noise in the darkness. The sound of the men's voices stopped. Euan struggled to lift the weight of the heavy end of the gate to ease it into place. Then he heard shouting and swearing and knew the clanging noise of the gate had alerted the thieves. He struggled frantically to get the gates together so that he could shove the bolts in place to hold them. One of the men yelled loudly.

'Get in! Get into the bloody Land Rover. Some bugger must have seen us. He's trying to shut us in!' Euan didn't hear the reply as he pulled and tugged, struggling to get the iron gates to meet so he could secure the bolts and then padlock the chain. He got the two gates together at last and managed to shoot one of the bolts as the Land Rover came round the corner at speed. The headlights blinded him as he wrestled with the other bolt. He didn't see the heavy bull bars on the front of the vehicle. Too late he realised the driver had no intention of stopping, or even slowing. They meant to burst the gates open. He tried to jump aside but his foot slipped. He clung to the gate to keep himself upright, sure now the driver would run over him if he fell to the ground.

'There's somebody there! Stop!' a voice shouted.

Euan was certain the driver must have seen him but he had no intention of stopping.

'Are ye mad? Ye'll kill him! Oh my God . . . '

The Land Rover, with the weight of the loaded trailer behind, crashed through the gates, bursting them apart easily while there was only the single bolt in place to hold them together. Euan felt a sharp pain in his arm before he was slammed, hard, back against the wall, pinioned there by the twisted metal of the gate. He was powerless to help himself. The loaded trailer skidded out of control. It swung precariously behind the Land Rover, battering the gate against the wall a second time, and Euan with it. Blackness descended.

'Ye hit somebody!' the other man gasped. 'Ye might have killed him. We'd better stop . . . '

'Shut yer bloody mouth. Ye said there was nobody in the farmhouse on Sunday nights!' the driver growled angrily. His companion didn't reply. He was terrified now. What if they had killed a man? He didn't like this job. He'd tried to tell Galt they'd done

216

enough in this area but he wouldn't listen — not after he heard of the special beef cattle at Ashburn.

They sped down the concrete yard. Headlights flashed on in front, blinding them. Galt uttered a stream of oaths as he stood on the brakes. The trailer slewed and jack-knifed. Pigs squealed with fear. The bonnet of the Land Rover came to a halt against the bottom gates. The noise of the squealing pigs was joined by that of a siren. Galt made to scramble out of his vehicle and make a dash for it. Then he saw the flashing blue lights and realised it was too late. He swore even more fluently than before. A second police car swerved to the left and parked on the far side of the Lennoxes' cottage, effectively cutting them off if they tried to make a break for it across the fields and down the back track. Galt turned and landed a furious punch at his accomplice's right eye, yelling every swear word he could call to mind, as well as a few inventions of his own.

While the police officers were dealing with the two men, Roseanne moved closer to Jock McItnyre. 'They must have got through the top gates,' she said in a low voice. 'I'm going to make sure Euan is all right. Even if he didn't manage to close them in time, I thought he would have been down here to see the men being arrested.'

'Aye.' Jock frowned. 'Aye, you do that, lassie. The police will want to talk to all of us. You stay at the house and I'll tell them where you are.'

Roseanne ran back up the yard. Every instinct told her something must be wrong or Euan would have joined them. Could they have fought with him? There were two of them. Was he hurt? It would be her fault if he had been injured. She should have shut the top gates herself. They were heavy, but there was a knack to dealing with them and she was more familiar with the way they worked.

Everything was still in darkness. She called Euan's name. There was no reply. She ran to the door of the house and switched on the lights inside and out. Her heart was thumping in alarm now. The yellow glow of the single outside bulb shone on the buckled gates just past the end of the house. The longest one was badly twisted.

Then she saw Euan lying in the shadows trapped between the gate and the wall. He lay still and silent. There was no response when she called his name. She could see at once that his head was bleeding badly. She managed to lift and tug the iron gate aside a little so she could squeeze behind it and reach him. She knelt beside him, whispering his name urgently, over and over, but there was no response. She drew his head into her lap and pulled out her mobile phone. Her fingers trembled as she dialled for an ambulance.

10

Roseanne was exhausted, but she refused to leave Euan's bedside once the doctors allowed her in to see him. She blamed herself for his accident. She should never have left him on his own to close the heavy top gates. Nothing Jock or his wife could say had made her feel any better. She didn't know how she was going to explain to Euan's mother and his Uncle Simon. He was in a single room at the local hospital and he was still unconscious with a nurse constantly in attendance. The doctors were debating whether he should be moved to Glasgow on account of his head injury. Even more frightening was the policeman waiting outside.

'If he dies it will be murder,' he said grimly, 'or manslaughter at least.'

Roseanne shuddered in horror. There

had been innumerable questions to answer, and even more when the police realised a man had been severely injured. She felt overwhelmed with guilt. Should she telephone Australia? It was already daylight here so night would be approaching over there. Should she let them have a night's sleep in peace and tell them at the start of their day? The nurse was a pleasant middle-aged woman, and Roseanne asked her advice.

'I think you should wait a while, dear. There's nothing they can do when they're on the other side o' the world, and twelve hours can make a big difference. We might have better news by then. It's never good to give bad news at bedtime, especially when the laddie's mother has been ill, as you said.'

Roseanne followed her advice. When another nurse came in to check the tubes, Roseanne pointed to Euan's left hand. 'His fingers are twisted. They're not usually like that. Are they broken?'

The nurse looked more closely. 'I

think they may be. His head injury was the priority, though. It still is. We're giving all our attention to that. He'll have a mighty sore head when he does come round.'

Roseanne had noticed a broad swath of Euan's thick dark hair had been shaved away, but his hair would grow again.

'Please God, make him well,' she whispered.

It seemed an age before the doctors came round again. The nurse had drawn attention to Euan's injured hand. The doctor nodded then insisted Roseanne should go home and get some rest. 'We have your telephone number and you may come back in the afternoon. We need to do some tests and attend to his broken leg. We shall keep you informed.'

Reluctantly Roseanne obeyed. She dreaded breaking the news to Euan's mother, and she needed to telephone Kershaw & Co. and let them know she would not be in, and prioritise the work as far as she could. She knew they would all do their best once they understood the seriousness of the situation, and they had her mobile number to keep in contact. She was putting the phone down with a huge sigh when Jock McIntyre called in to ask how Euan was. She was sure she could neither eat not sleep, but Jock had other ideas.

'Ye look exhausted, lassie,' he remarked when she'd finished telling him Euan had not regained consciousness. 'Ye'll be no use to him if ye dinnae get something to eat and then have a rest. I'm going to wait here until ye've made some porridge. There's plenty o' cream on top o' the milk I brought up for ye earlier.'

Roseanne grimaced but she obeyed. She knew her churning stomach would feel better for having some food to digest. She couldn't go to bed but she compromised by stretching out on the long settee with the telephone close at hand.

She couldn't believe it was two o'clock in the afternoon when she wakened. She had a quick shower and changed her clothes. She ate some toast and a cup of coffee but she was desperate to get back to the hospital and see Euan for herself.

The policeman had gone and the room was empty. Roseanne's heart thumped with fear. She hurried to the nurses' station and her knees almost buckled with relief when they told her he had been moved to another side ward. She found there was another patient there too and a nurse keeping checks on both of them. Surely that must be a better sign?

'He regained consciousness briefly but the doctors are keeping him heavily sedated,' the nurse explained. 'His back and shoulders are badly bruised, and he has two fractures to his left leg and two broken fingers.'

'This is terrible,' Roseanne groaned.

'The broken bones will heal and the bruising will disappear in time. The doctors are more concerned about his head injury. He lost a lot of blood. He kept muttering about roses. He became agitated when we didn't understand so we had to sedate him.'

'Er . . . my name is Roseanne. Could that be what he was saying?'

'It might have been,' the nurse said thoughtfully, her eyes widening. 'We told him the roses were fine and gave him another injection. Rest and sleep will do him more good than anything at present.'

Roseanne sat quietly by the bed. Euan's eyes were closed and she marvelled at the thick, dark crescents his eyelashes made on his pale cheeks. He looked so young and vulnerable lying there in the hospital bed. Her heart filled with a strange tenderness as she watched over him.

Just before seven o'clock her patience was rewarded. Euan opened his eyes. She was deeply thankful when he recognised her.

'Roseanne . . . ?' he murmured.

'Where are we?'

'In hospital,' Roseanne said huskily, and her eyes filled with tears. She never cried but she felt weak with relief. She brushed the tears away and leaned forward to kiss his cheek. 'Thank God you've regained consciousness, Euan.' She was holding his right hand in both of hers. She felt a faint pressure as he tried to squeeze her fingers. Perspiration began to coat his forehead though and the nurse asked her to move away.

'It's the pain and the medication,' she said gently. 'We shall keep him sedated until it eases. It is going to take some time, but he is going to be all right.'

'You're sure?'

'Well, the doctors are much happier about him now than when he was first brought in.'

Roseanne gave her a wobbly smile. She bent to kiss Euan again.

'I shall be close by,' she whispered. 'Sleep now.'

Later, Roseanne telephoned Mr K to give him a full report.

226

'Hey, Roseanne, are you crying? I haven't known you to weep since you were six years old, lassie. You mustn't blame yourself. Euan is a grown man. His mother says he's always had a mind of his own. He would know what he was doing.'

'Oh Uncle K, he could have been killed. I feel so guilty. He looks so helpless and defenceless lying there in hospital.'

'Ah lassie, there's no need to feel guilty.' He smiled to himself in spite of her distressing news. Roseanne had always called him Uncle K until she came to work at Kershaw's, then she had decided she must address him as Mr K like the rest of his staff. She had never wanted any special treatment but he had missed her affectionate address.

'Shall I give you the telephone number of the hospital? I'm sure Euan's mother will want to telephone to get first-hand news from the doctor. I'm no relation so they won't tell me any details.'

'Aye, I'll write it down.' He lowered his voice. 'I reckon she might decide to come over to see him.'

'Oh dear . . . '

'Don't fret, Roseanne. She's been talking about coming back with me for a holiday anyway. Between ourselves, lassie, I'm ready for home. If Aileen will come with me now it would suit me fine. She's keeping better than I expected. She says she feels better than she has done for years so I think it might be the best thing all round if we can get a flight.'

* * *

As soon as he had fully regained his senses, and the pain had abated somewhat, Euan began pestering the nurses, wanting to get out of hospital.

'Didn't you say he was supposed to be on holiday for three months?' one of them grumbled.

'He is,' Roseanne assured her, 'and he has finished the work he was doing for our firm. The new system is working splendidly so he has no worries there.' She had been relieved to discover the new computer system at Kershaw & Co. allowed her to access some of her work from Ashburn, once she had explained to Louise what she needed her to do.

'He keeps saying he has to get out of here because he's wasting precious time and he only has another week. He says it will be too late after that. The only time he calms down is when you come in to visit.'

'I'm sorry,' Roseanne apologised. 'I come as often as I can but our boss is still away in Australia, so I need to keep going back to supervise the business. That shouldn't worry Euan though.'

'Well something is bothering him,' the nurse insisted. 'He was muttering about the girl he wanted to marry going off with another man.'

'I see,' Roseanne said slowly, frowning. 'I'm afraid I don't know anything about that, but I haven't known him very long.'

'Oh?' The nurse looked surprised. 'We thought he meant you, though I must say you don't look the sort who would take advantage and go off with somebody else while a man is ill.'

'No, he couldn't have meant me,' Roseanne said, puzzled. 'His mother and uncle are returning from Australia soon, so perhaps that will cheer him up a bit. I shall not be here so often then.'

'He's a lot easier managed when you've been in to see him,' the nurse said. 'Maybe he's just missing not having his friends over here.'

'Maybe,' Roseanne murmured, but she had seen how all the nurses tumbled over themselves to attend to him and how they bloomed whenever he gave them a smile.

Euan's back and shoulders were still badly bruised, and the doctors had told him he was lucky not to have a broken shoulder and more serious injuries to his spine, so Roseanne had some sympathy for him over that.

Everyone at Kershaw & Co. did their best to co-operate. They understood how difficult it was for Roseanne to take Mr K's place during his absence as well as finding time to spend with his nephew down in the Borders, especially when he was a stranger in an unfamiliar country. Then there was her new flat to sort out before Robinia arrived.

Roseanne drove down to Ashburn as soon as she could get away on Friday, planning to stay until Monday morning. She wanted to make the most of the weekend and spend the time with Euan. He had a room of his own again and the staff were very lenient over visiting times. Roseanne was surprised to find they had so many things in common now they had plenty of time and opportunity to talk on neutral ground, but they still enjoyed a stimulating discussion now and then. Euan was restless. He protested whenever she had to leave. He always pleaded for what he called a proper kiss from her, even if she was only leaving for a short time while he had his meals and medication.

'You're taking advantage of my soft heart,' Roseanne teased. 'You know I'm only complying to your demands because I still feel guilty about you getting hurt.'

'Oh God, that's the last thing I want,' he groaned, his brow darkening. 'I'd rather you never came at all than come because you feel guilty, especially when you have no cause to feel that way.'

'I see,' Roseanne said uncertainly. 'Well if you'd rather I didn't come . . . '

'Of course I don't mean that. I do want you to come, but I don't want you to visit me because it eases your conscience, Roseanne. I want you to come because it is what you want to do. Preferably because you can't survive without seeing me . . . ?' he said, his tone lightening, teasing a little, but there was a strangely vulnerable look in his eyes and Roseanne's heart lurched with tenderness.

'Of course I want to come and see you. In fact I have enjoyed our discussions while you have been in here. I find it interesting hearing about the projects you've handled and the countries you've visited.'

'And there was I thinking you were at last succumbing to my charms,' Euan said with a grin.

'All the nurses are doing enough of that without me adding to the list,' Roseanne quipped. Euan knew he couldn't tell her how badly he missed her company. He always waited impatiently for her return.

'I can't tell you how much I appreciate you spending your free time with me, Roseanne,' he said. He repeated this in many different ways so she knew he was sincere, but she also knew he was getting better when he began to hold her close with his good arm so that he could prolong each kiss far longer than any casual leave-taking.

He had asked for his laptop. The doctors refused at first, but they realised he was bored and that was a sign of recovery, so they relented on the condition he did not use it for lengthy periods and aggravate the headaches, which were still causing some concern.

'I promise not to be a pest, but I want to keep in touch with you every single day, Roseanne. Can I email you if I restrict myself to one a day?'

'Of course you can,' Roseanne responded readily, pleased that he seemed to miss her and that he wanted to keep in daily contact. 'You will be discreet though?' she prompted, remembering their emails would all go through the central computer now, even though she doubted if Simon Kershaw would bother to read any of them.

'I'll try.' He grinned up at her, knowing they were both recalling the first time he had read her email. His smile faded. She had been writing to the unknown Rob. He'd almost forgotten about him and about the time passing. Was he there, sharing the flat now? Were they sharing her bed? He didn't want to think about that. If they didn't mention him, he could block the fellow out of his mind, especially since Roseanne was still spending every weekend with him. He was thankful for that.

★　★　★

Simon Kershaw had lost no time in booking flights back to the UK when the doctors eventually agreed his sister was fit to travel. He visited Euan at the first opportunity and told him his mother would visit as soon as she had recovered from the journey. Euan was pleased to see him.

'I think they may let me out of this place as soon as my mother is able to visit. I shall tell them there is someone at home to look after me — though really I should be looking after her. How is she really, Uncle Simon? Has she fully recovered from her operation?'

'The doctors gave her the all clear,' Simon told him, 'and she says she feels better than she has felt for years. It's the travelling, really, and she's been anxious about you, so it's tired her out. Anyway, I'm sure Roseanne will have been looking after you. She feels guilty for letting you get injured.'

'I don't want her to visit me because she feels guilty,' Euan said, frowning. 'Besides, my injuries were not her fault,' he added.

'I don't think they'll allow you home anyway until they're sure you're right in the head, laddie.'

Euan grinned at his uncle's turn of phrase. 'Some people might think I've never been right in the head.' He sobered. 'The headaches are not as severe now, or as often. So long as I don't do too much bending I think I can cope with them.'

'Well your mother reckons you usually get your own way, so I expect you'll pester these nurses until they let you out. I need to get back up to the factory and see what's going on and relieve Roseanne a bit, give her a bit of time off to get settled into her new flat.'

Roseanne felt she ought not to intrude now Euan's uncle and mother had arrived back at Ashburn and were visiting him every day. He was dismayed when he realised she would not be coming down the following weekend as usual. His spirits plummeted. While he was ill and sedated he had lost track of time, but now he faced facts. The unknown Rob must certainly be living at the flat by now. No doubt he was glad Roseanne no longer needed to spend her precious free time visiting her employer's nephew.

Euan was aware Roseanne still blamed herself for his injuries, despite his protests. He had taken advantage of her feelings to make the most of her company. He had lived for the weekends, when she would be back to see him and she had answered all his emails once he got his computer at the hospital, but he felt he must face the fact that guilt was probably the only emotion she had felt where he was concerned. Obviously it was the reason she had spent her precious weekends visiting him, especially since he knew no one else in Scotland. If her feelings had been deeper she would not have stayed away as soon as he had his mother and uncle to visit.

Euan was enjoying getting to know his uncle and learning more about the workings of the meat processing operations, but he was bored and despondent now he could no longer look forward to Roseanne's visits.

'The doctor says Euan has had a setback since we arrived,' Simon Kershaw told Roseanne. 'We thought it would help him, having his mother to visit every afternoon, but she says he seems moody and withdrawn and the doctors think it is too soon to discharge him in case his head injuries are more severe than they thought.'

'Are they sure he hasn't developed an infection in one of his wounds? Has his head injury healed properly?'

'I reckon the doctors will know about

all that. They think he's been spending too much time on his computer. He seems to be in contact with colleagues all over the globe.'

'I suppose he misses his own friends,' Roseanne said, chewing her lower lip. She longed to go down and see him for herself, but she owed her loyalty to Robinia too. She was now installed at the flat, but she had been restless ever since she arrived. Roseanne felt torn between her work, her sister and Euan. She had no excuse for spending weekends at Ashburn now, though. Robinia was used to having plenty of people around her, and she was not accustomed to staying in one place for long. Even so, Roseanne had a feeling there was more than that affecting her sister's spirits and she wondered if she was regretting tying up her money in the new flat and giving up her job to take over one of their mother's boutiques and start making her own name in the retail world. Her job had meant she was continually on the move and meeting new people. Giving it all up meant a big change to her lifestyle. Their mother had thought the sisters should spend some time together before Robinia took over the boutique, but Roseanne was beginning to think the sooner Rob had something to occupy her time and energy the better.

'There'll be no need for you to keep rushing down to Ashburn now that the Hunk's mother has arrived,' Robinia said with satisfaction when she heard Mr K and his sister had returned from Australia.

'I'm not sure Mrs Kennedy would welcome me there anyway,' Roseanne said. 'I can't blame her if she holds me responsible for Euan's injuries.'

'Don't be silly, Ros,' Robinia said briskly. 'No one can blame you. Euan Kennedy most definitely has a mind of his own from what you tell me. Now cheer up. We'll spend your first free Saturday shopping together and maybe have Sunday afternoon with Mother.'

Roseanne smiled in response to her

sister's suggestions but inwardly her spirits felt unusually low and she knew it was the prospect of not knowing if, or when, she would see Euan again. Simon Kershaw had told her Euan's mother visited the hospital every afternoon but she had refused to drive Euan's sports car. She had already bought a small car of her own so that she could be independent and drive herself to the shops or the hospital when it suited her.

'It sounds as though she's planning to stay indefinitely,' Robinia said with satisfaction when Roseanne told her the news. 'Maybe she'll settle in this country.'

Mr K was happy to be back in harness but he divided his time between the factory and his sister at Ashburn for the first couple of weeks. He had known both Robinia and Roseanne since they were children, so he guessed Roseanne would feel she should spend some time with her restless sibling. He knew Robinia had always made her base with her mother in the past if she was in

Britain for any length of time, but Roseanne had told him they had bought the new flat between them and Robinia had moved all her personal possessions from her mother's down to the flat. It seemed she was intending to make her home permanently with Roseanne. Simon Kershaw frowned at that prospect, although it was none of his business. He knew the two of them had always been close in spite of the differences in their temperaments, but he knew better than anyone how much Roseanne valued her own space and privacy. He wondered how they would get on living together, and whether Robinia would be bored staying in a small town, even if she did travel to Edinburgh every day.

Roseanne also wondered. She spent as much time at the flat as she could but she sensed that her sister was not happy. When questioned she replied sharply, 'I've scarcely seen you, what with your work and the time you've spent visiting your precious hunk. When will he be well enough for us to try some of our old tricks on him?'

'I don't think we should try anything when he has been so ill,' Roseanne said quickly. Robinia looked up at her swift response. She eyed her sister thoughtfully. She knew Roseanne well enough to realise Euan Kennedy must be more special than her usual male friends. She had never been so attentive, or so protective, with anyone before. Rob was beginning to suspect it was more than guilt, or a sense of responsibility, which made her sister so concerned and attentive. This must be a man who mattered. Robinia couldn't remember her elder sister ever being deeply attached to anyone before, except family and Uncle K. She might say she felt responsible for Euan's accident, she might blame herself and convince everyone she owed him a debt; but Robinia knew there was more to her sister's feelings than that, whether Roseanne realised it or not. Maybe she was seeing things more clearly herself.

For the first time in her life she understood now what true love really meant, and it was not all laughter and having a good time together as she had once imagined . . .

11

'Euan keeps asking when you're coming down to Ashburn for the weekend,' Simon Kershaw told Roseanne as another weekend approached. 'Could you manage to come, lassie, even if it's only for a night? I think he needs some young company to cheer him up. He gets on well with young McIntyre. They talk about computer programs and suchlike but it's not the same. Surely Binny can amuse herself for once?' he asked.

Roseanne smiled. He had always called her sister Binny when they were children. All shortened forms of their names annoyed their mother, but Rob herself had refused to answer to Binny since she had become a successful model. 'It makes me sound like a dustbin man,' she declared.

'Well yes, I suppose I could come

down for the day on Saturday,' Roseanne agreed slowly. 'Rob seems to be in brighter spirits this week for some reason. I don't want to intrude at Ashburn, though, when your sister is staying there.'

'But Ashburn is your home, lassie. It is where your heart belongs. I've always known that. If Aileen decides to stay in Scotland — and I hope she will — then she thinks she will settle up here, nearer my work. When Euan is better, she'll probably move into the empty flat while she looks around for a place. Anyway, she is eager to meet you. She'll be as pleased as I am if you come to Ashburn. Better still if you stay all weekend. Besides, the cattle records are getting behind,' he added with a twinkle in his eye. 'You know I can never understand that damned computer program the government insist we must use to register all the births.'

Roseanne explained to her sister about needing to go to Ashburn to catch up with the cattle records.

Robinia smiled and gave her a quizzical look.

'It's not worth going all that way for one night. Why don't you go on Friday and come back Monday morning?' Roseanne was astonished at her sister's suggestion.

'If I didn't know better I'd think you were trying to get me out of the way,' Roseanne teased. She was surprised when Robinia's cheeks coloured. 'Why don't you come with me?'

'Not on your life. You know I never liked staying at the farm. I admit I've been a bit grumpy since I came home. I wondered if I was doing the right thing buying this flat with you, committing both of us to a substantial mortgage, as well as giving up a job I've loved.'

'And now? Are you still unsure?' Roseanne asked anxiously. 'I'd hate you to be unhappy, Rob.'

'I think things are going to work out better than I could have believed,' Robinia said, with a dreamy sort of smile Roseanne had never seen before.

'You said Euan would be getting out of hospital soon, didn't you?'

'Yes. If the tests are all satisfactory he expects to get out next Thursday, so long as there is someone to keep an eye on him.'

Roseanne raised her eyebrows at her sister's speculative gaze, unaware that Robinia was making mental plans of her own. So far Rob had not mentioned her own particular friend, Jonathan Weston, to Roseanne but if she had the flat to herself for the whole weekend they could stay here together. He had landed back in Edinburgh three days ago. She hadn't realised how unhappy and restless she had been until he phoned her from the airport to say he had arrived in Scotland and couldn't wait to see her. She had travelled up to town as soon as Roseanne left for work the following day, and again the next, arriving back just before her sister got home from work. She couldn't explain why she wanted to keep Jonathan a secret, except that she cared for him more deeply than she had ever cared for any man in her life before. Until she heard his voice and felt the warmth of his embrace again she had been filled with doubts. Even now, she wondered if she was being selfish to allow Jonathan to give up a job he loved as a fashion photographer just because the time was coming when she would be giving up her own career as a model. Her mother was getting older, and several times she had hinted that running all three boutiques was too much for her on her own. She had been delighted when Robinia agreed it was time to quit her modelling career while she was still in demand, and take over one of the boutiques. She had also promised to help with the buying for all three boutiques, and she knew this was the part she would really enjoy.

When she had first explained to Jonathan that she was buying a flat with her sister he hadn't seemed bothered, but when he realised she would also be giving up her modelling and settling down to run a boutique in Edinburgh he had gone very quiet. He had barely spoken to her for days. She had been so miserable. They cared deeply about each other. They were good together, as friends and as lovers. She had asked herself a dozen times since arriving home if she was a fool to throw it all away before she was forced into changes. It was true Jonathan had insisted on accompanying her to the airport, and when she was almost ready to board the plane he had taken her in his arms and told her he didn't think he could live his life without her. She knew he had meant it at the time, but afterwards she'd had time to ponder. Saying goodbye was always emotional. Would he still feel the same when she had been out of his life for a few weeks? Now here he was in Scotland, asking her to marry him, planning to change his own job and set up in a business of his own so that they could settle down together. She simply couldn't believe all her dreams were coming true. Jonathan would have no difficulty getting other photographic work because he had built up a large portfolio and he had an excellent reputation with the glossy magazines both in the UK and abroad. Her big worry now was the flat she and Roseanne had bought together so recently.

Her mother had been adamant it was her duty to encourage Roseanne to buy a bigger and better flat, in a more residential area, but her elder sister had always kept her affairs to herself so neither of them had any idea whether she could afford a more expensive place. As usual, Robinia had gone along with her mother's suggestions, but she had not known then that her decision to settle down would set so many other changes in motion. The flat was lovely. How could she expect Roseanne to put it on the market again so soon? How else could she sort out the new complications which would arise if she married Jonathan? Yet, she knew now, that was what she wanted more than anything else.

★ ★ ★

Roseanne was delighted to discover Aileen Kennedy resembled her brother both in looks and nature. She greeted her with a warm hug as though they had known each other for years.

'I feel I know you, Roseanne,' she said with a smile. 'I've heard so much about you from Simon. I believe he regards you as the daughter he never had.'

'Thank you. He has been very good to me since my grandfather died.'

'From what I hear, you have more than repaid him with your help and loyalty. He tells me you have a business brain as sharp as your grandfather had.'

'I suppose things have turned out to be to our mutual benefit,' Roseanne agreed. 'I'd have hated having to sell the farm but I couldn't have made it pay on its own.'

'But together the two places make a viable unit?'

'Yes, they do, and it has been good for the reputation of Kershaw & Co. to have some organic meat from our rare breeds. It seems to make a difference to some of the large London stores. A marketing image you know. How is Euan progressing?'

'He's looking forward to seeing you. I know he sends you an email every day but he says that's very restricting.' She gave Roseanne a shrewd look which brought the ready colour to her cheeks.

'I, er . . . I expect he means we can't argue in emails.'

'Maybe that's what he meant, though I don't think so. I do know he has enjoyed some stimulating discussions with you. He's impatient to get out of hospital now that I'm here to keep an eye on him and he's feeling so much better. The headaches have almost gone and I gather they were what caused concern and why the doctors insisted on keeping him in for observation.'

Roseanne was surprised when Euan's mother and uncle both opted out of visiting while she was at Ashburn.

'I told you, he's needing some young company, lassie. There's not much fun in seeing two old fogies like us,' Simon Kershaw said with a grin.

Euan was sitting in a chair by the window when Roseanne arrived. He still had a room to himself which surprised her. He also had an extra table and chair with his computer set up ready for use.

'How did you manage all this?' she asked, gesturing around the room.

'Oh a few strings here and there did the trick,' Euan said, waving dismissively. 'I suppose there's an advantage in being in a small local hospital where rules can be bent a bit. But never mind the room. Surely I deserve a greeting from you. I haven't seen you since my mother arrived.' He beckoned her closer and clasped her hand the moment he could reach it. She was surprised how strong he was as he drew her close and lifted his face for a kiss. As soon as she bent towards him he put his hand to the back of her head while his lips sought hers in a long kiss which left them both breathless.

'You're certainly recovering,' Roseanne gasped, blushing furiously.

'I have not forgotten how quick and cool your kisses can be, Roseanne. I have to make the most of any opportunity which comes my way,' Euan teased, grinning broadly. 'How long can you stay?'

'Until the end of visiting, unless you turn me out,' Roseanne said, but her green eyes danced with mischief and Euan felt his heart lurch. God he wanted her.

'You know very well I meant how many days will you be at Ashburn.'

'I'm staying until Monday morning and driving straight back to the office from Ashburn.'

'And Rob doesn't mind you being away so long?' he asked carefully, his eyes never leaving her face.

'Apparently not.' Roseanne shrugged, her thoughts flitting back to her sister. Robinia was up to something. She had always been able to tell, but so far she had been unable to work out what it could be. She knew Rob had been up to town at least once this past week, because their mother had telephoned Roseanne at work to say she had seen her walking past the boutique with a man. But they had not called to see her, and they had disappeared by the time she was able to leave her client.

She looked up to see Euan frowning at her. He didn't care for her going off into a reverie at the mere mention of the unknown Rob. He vowed he must make the most of the little time and opportunity he had.

'What have you been doing with your computer?' she asked. 'Apart from sending me emails?'

'I have to restrict myself where you're concerned, remembering how scrupulous you are about personal emails at work — we-ell . . . most of the time!'

His grey eyes lit with golden flecks and she knew he was remembering the private email she had sent off to Rob which he had intercepted when he had first arrived. 'I do love the colour in your cheeks, Roseanne.' He chuckled and Roseanne wished she didn't blush so readily.

'So what else do you need your computer for? It looks very up to date.'

'Of course it is. What else would you expect considering my business is computers? As a matter of fact, I have been able to keep in touch with most of the projects my company are working on, and things are going very well. I'm making plans for some major changes.'

'I see. I suppose that means you will be moving on as soon as the doctors give you the all-clear?' Roseanne couldn't believe how depressed that made her feel. They would probably never see each other again once he resumed his travelling far and wide. When the bell rang for the end of visiting time her kiss was more lingering than usual and Euan made the most of it.

'You will come back again this evening, won't you, Roseanne?' he asked, and her heart filled with tenderness at the vulnerable look in his eyes. She felt like a mother deserting her child as she turned back to wave from the door. Her heart ached. She was going to miss him terribly when he was fully recovered.

They both made the most of each visiting time during the weekend. On Sunday evening when she was ready to leave, Euan mentioned again that he had some serious decisions to make regarding his own business but Roseanne was too preoccupied to pay attention. Their parting kiss was long and passionate, only brought to an end by the gentle cough of the nurse.

It was only later, lying in bed, that she wondered what he had meant about his business. What had he been trying to say? She knew he was restless and often irritable on account of his lack of mobility. He had said there was still a lot to discuss before anything could be arranged. 'I need to get on my feet again for one thing,' he had muttered impatiently. As soon as his leg was healed and he had had the physiotherapy he would be off on his travels. Roseanne's heart filled with despair. She would probably never see him again once he resumed his own projects.

*   *   *

When Roseanne arrived home from work on Monday evening she was feeling flat and depressed. She didn't want to face Rob's teasing questions about Euan and the weekend, so she fired off a few questions of her own instead.

'Have you been to Edinburgh again today to meet your current boyfriend?' she asked, taking her sister by surprise as she had intended.

'How do you know about that?' Rob asked.

'Mother told me she had seen you one afternoon last week. Is he the Jonathan you mentioned so often when you were doing assignments together?' she asked.

'Ye-es . . . ' Rob admitted slowly. 'He's a photographer. We worked together most of the time during the past nine months, but we've known each other almost since we both began in the fashion industry.'

'Did he like our new flat?' Roseanne asked innocently.

'How do you know he's seen it?' Robinia asked quickly.

'I saw his aftershave in the bathroom.' Roseanne grinned at her sister's frown.

'There's no hiding anything from you, is there?'

'Not a lot. I suspect there must be something special about this Jonathan? You've never brought any of your other men to stay.'

'Yes, he is special. He's different. Oh Roseanne, I really care about him, just as you said I would one day,' Rob confessed, her blush deepening. 'I'm almost afraid to introduce him to you and Mother.'

'He matters so much? Are we likely to disillusion him?'

'He might prefer you to me when he meets you. Looks wouldn't count for anything because we're so alike, but Jonathan has a more serious outlook on life, and you two would have a lot in common. As for Mother, you know what she's like for questioning people about their prospects,' she added dryly. 'I mean, in this day and age men don't expect to be vetted by a future mother-in-law, do they?'

'I wouldn't know. Does that mean you are thinking about marriage then? It's that serious?'

'Yes,' Robinia said in a small voice. 'We're thinking of having a quiet wedding in a registry office, then telling everyone afterwards. I hadn't really meant to tell you that but you took me by surprise. Would you be terribly hurt, Ros?' Rob looked at her anxiously.

'No-o, I suppose not, if it's what you both want, but I would like to meet him before you took such a serious step. I'm sure Mother would be disappointed though. You know how proud she is of your glamorous lifestyle. She'd love arranging a wedding and making you the bride of the year. Besides it would be good publicity for you taking over the boutique.'

'If Mother is so proud of me, why does she keep telling me I should be more like you?' Rob asked, almost accusingly.

'Like me? She wouldn't want two of me. She's always telling me I should pay more attention to my appearance and make more of myself, as you do.'

'Our mother is a wretch!' Rob said, almost angrily. 'She persuaded me to help you buy this flat because she said yours was in the wrong area and too small to give you any status. As though you need status with all your assets and brilliant career,' she scoffed. 'But she wouldn't listen.'

'I believe you,' Roseanne said dryly. 'The angle she used with me was that you frittered away all your money. She insisted that if I would buy a half share in a decent flat with you it would compel you to save some money and give you an investment for your future. She came down to inspect it, you know, before I signed on the dotted line.'

'Well!' Rob exclaimed indignantly. 'I've never frittered away my money. How could I after the way she brought us up? She worked so hard after Daddy died.'

'I know,' Roseanne said quietly. 'She must have had a struggle. She can't get used to not being in charge of everything we do — like doling out our pocket money and withholding it if we're naughty. She still likes to feel she has some control over us still, so she resorts to being a bit devious.'

'I suppose she means well,' Rob

agreed with a sigh. 'So, you think Jonathan and I shouldn't get married in secret? You think Mother will be mortally wounded?'

'I think you should at least introduce Jonathan to Mother. I'd like to meet him too, preferably before you get engaged — or were you planning to cut out that step?'

'I don't know. I'll discuss it with him,' Rob promised. 'Speaking of meeting, I'd like a look at your Euan now he's nearly recovered.'

'He's not my Euan,' Roseanne denied hastily, too hastily for a sister who knew her so well. Rob looked amused as she watched Roseanne's cheeks fire up. 'Anyway, if he gets out of hospital this next week he'll be more independent. He'll probably not need me to visit.'

It was clear to Rob that her big sister was eager to see Euan whether or not he needed her. She didn't want to play their old pranks on him either. That could mean only one thing — Roseanne really cared for Euan Kennedy.

Rob frowned. Was he worthy of her beloved sister, or would he forget her as soon as he was well enough to resume his travels and take up his own affairs again? Rob couldn't bear the thought of Roseanne being let down and hurt. Although they grumbled between themselves when their mother tried to organise them, the three of them had always looked out for each other. Rob decided she would like to meet Euan Kennedy and see what kind of man he was. It would be easier to pay him a short visit while he was still in hospital, rather than wait until he was convalescing at the farm. There was no time to lose if he was to be discharged soon.

Rob travelled down to the hospital the following morning, without telling Roseanne of her plans. She would have lunch in the town and arrive early for afternoon visiting, in case Euan's mother visited too. She was wearing the navy trouser suit she had worn to fly home and she had plaited her long auburn hair and coiled it around her neatly shaped head in the same style which Roseanne wore when she was working. She had not done it with the conscious intention of playing their old tricks on Euan Kennedy. When they had pretended to take each other's identity in the past they had both been teenagers and they had swapped clothes and agreed on a plot together, usually to give a persistent or arrogant young man his come-uppance, but as she caught a glimpse of herself in the long windows Rob almost believed it was Roseanne looking back at her.

Euan was sitting in a chair looking out of the window with a pair of crutches beside him and a pile of books and his computer on a table. When Robinia walked into the room she saw his eyes light up in welcome.

'This is a lovely surprise, Roseanne,' he said, holding out his hand in eager greeting, beckoning her close. He held up his face for a kiss. Robinia hesitated for a fraction of a second, realising he thought she was Roseanne, then she bent and kissed him fully on the mouth. Robinia never did things by half. Euan blinked. His spirits rose.

'How did you wangle an extra day? Is Uncle Simon taking over for once?'

'Something like that,' Robinia murmured, only now beginning to realise this might not be such a good idea. It was one thing to play tricks with Roseanne's co-operation when they filled each other in on what to say and do, or not, but it was quite another to act in secret. Roseanne and Euan had spent a lot of time together in recent weeks. What did they discuss? How intimate had they become? She began to talk about the flat. Euan listened, puzzled. Had she forgotten he'd seen the flat several times when he helped her to move? There was something wrong, something different. A vague memory teased at his mind.

'I've been in touch with two of my business colleagues,' he said. 'They're going to discuss my proposition to sell each of them a quarter of my company. As soon as I'm well enough to travel to London we'll have a meeting. Will you come with me, Roseanne?'

'If you want me to.' Robinia smiled uncertainly, but she was sure her sister would be willing to go with him. He was certainly a good-looking man and he had a most attractive smile. She wondered why he was selling off his company, or at least a large part of it. Was he short of money? She frowned and scrutinized his face. Surely he couldn't be after Roseanne's share in Kershaw's. Euan wondered why she was studying him so intently.

'Who else would I ask to accompany me? You have the business skills and training to advise me.'

'Oh, so it's only my knowledge you want?' Robinia asked, but she fluttered her thick lashes at him. Was she flirting with him? Euan's eyes widened. Roseanne didn't flirt, and she never wore so much mascara or that green eye shadow. He looked more closely. He clasped her hand, stroking her palm with his thumb. Roseanne always reacted to that particular touch. Today he could have been stroking the bedpost. He turned her hand over and studied her nails, carefully manicured, painted with purple nail varnish. His eyes narrowed. Roseanne never painted her nails when she was working in case she was called to one of the food processing plants, and he had never seen her with such brightly coloured nails. Could this be her sister? How alike they were. They could have been twins. He had a brief recollection of Jock McIntyre telling him how the sisters had often swapped places to play tricks on at least one young man. Had Roseanne agreed to play a trick on him? If so, why?

'You know I admire your business expertise,' he said smoothly, although his brain was racing. Something didn't add up. 'I need you to help me work out a fair deal for all of us.' His voice deepened deliberately. 'You must know

I want what will be best for us. For the future, Roseanne?' He slid her a sideways glance.

'I — er, yes, of course,' Robinia said, but she had no idea what Euan was talking about or how far she was committing her sister. Euan looked down at her hand as it lay in his. He looked up and saw her gaze was fixed on the view. He studied her intently. His brain was whirring.

'Your hair seems shorter. It doesn't quite meet.' He frowned. It had more blond streaks, now that he looked closely.

'I — er, often get the ends cut off. It makes it look thicker.' Robinia saw his intent stare. She knew he was beginning to suspect she was not Roseanne. Should she come clean? 'I — er, I think I'd better be going now.' His grip on her hand tightened.

'This is a very short visit. You can't go yet.'

'Er . . . I wanted to pop in to make sure you're all right. I must be getting back.'

'Why shouldn't I be all right? Except I can't wait to get out of this place, but you know that already.'

'When do they plan to discharge you?'

'Wednesday.' He gave the wrong day deliberately. It was the first thing Roseanne had asked on Friday evening. She never forgot details like that, especially when she knew how important it was to him. She bent to kiss him goodbye. Her perfume was different too, stronger, not Roseanne's light flowery scent. As soon as she was out of sight he reached for his crutches and swung himself along to where the windows overlooked the visitors' car park. There she was, with her long legs and the graceful walk he so admired. His heart skipped a beat at the sight of her, but she was not getting into her little blue car. He stared as she climbed into the driver's seat of a sporty yellow model. He knew for sure then he'd just had a visit from Roseanne's sister. He couldn't believe how alike they looked.

Why hadn't Roseanne warned him she would be coming? Or had she agreed to the deception?

Robinia heaved a huge sigh of relief. She should have told him who she was as soon as he kissed her and she realised he had mistaken her for Roseanne. She was still not sure whether Euan Kennedy would make Roseanne happy. He was certainly a good-looking guy, but her sister needed more than looks to satisfy her. She was not the type to go travelling the world with him either, especially if they had children. Roseanne would want stability. She felt uneasy at visiting him without her Ros's permission.

Euan muttered under his breath. There was something phoney going on. He remembered that first email at Kershaw & Co., and his encounter with Roseanne. Even then the sparks had flown between them like ice and fire, attracted and repelled; attracted again with an almighty fizz when they had spent the weekend at Ashburn, then the icy anger over the blasted entries in the company bank statement. But what was it she had written in the email?

' . . . *I'd say he's been around a bit. Perhaps it's time we played our old tricks again and had a bit of fun.*' He had assumed that email had been to a man called Rob. He'd assumed he was Roseanne's boyfriend. She had not contradicted him, then or later. He recalled the pangs of envy he had felt, and still felt, at the mere thought of them together.

Had Roseanne arranged for her sister to visit him today? Was she a party to the trick? She had to be. He was more hurt by her subterfuge than he cared to admit. They were having fun at his expense. He frowned. He had believed he and Roseanne had moved on rapidly during the last few weeks. They had explored each other's minds and he had believed Roseanne enjoyed his company and their discussions as much as he had enjoyed hers. Had she simply spent so much time with him because she still felt responsible for his accident?

When his mother and Uncle Simon came to visit that evening they found him unusually morose.

'You told me Roseanne has a sister. What's her name?' he asked abruptly.

'Her name?' Uncle Simon looked surprised. 'Why, Binny, of course.'

'I don't know why you always called her that,' his mother interrupted. 'Robinia is such a pretty name.'

'Robinia?' Euan asked sharply.

'Och, she gets all sorts of names. She uses her full name for her modelling, I believe, but Roseanne calls her Rob,' Uncle Simon said. 'They were christened Robinia and Roseanne after some flowers or shrubs or something. Their mother was into gardening at the time. There's only ten or eleven months between them. They were like two peas in a pod when they were wee girls,' he went on, reminiscing. 'Always up to tricks.'

'Are they still alike?' Euan asked.

'I suppose so, in looks anyway, but

not when you get to know them. Robinia hardly ever comes down to Ashburn, so I've not seen her for a while. She never liked the farm and smelly animals.'

'I see.'

'Why d'ye ask, Euan?'

'It was just something Jock McIntyre mentioned,' he prevaricated, 'about Roseanne playing a trick on some local fellow, a manager on one of the estates.'

'Ah, he'd be talking about Lord Gallaby's manager.' He chuckled. 'He was getting more serious than Roseanne wanted and he wouldn't believe her when she tried to break it off. Binny took her place one evening and led him on quite a bit, I believe. He asked her to marry him before he realised he'd got the wrong sister. She led him a merry dance. He was a conceited young pup, though, or they wouldn't have played a trick like that on him. He's never had much sense of humour either. If you ask me, he still has a fancy for Roseanne, but she needs more of a man than he'll ever be.'

★　★　★

Euan was thankful to get out of hospital, but he couldn't forget Robinia's visit. It nagged at him. Had Roseanne agreed to it? Had she arranged it? Why would she play a trick on him? Did she want rid of him, as she had Lord Gallaby's manager?

His heart went cold. Did she think he was getting too serious? Was he going too fast for her? It was true they had not known each other very long. He still didn't know the meaning of the entries in the firm's bank reconciliation, but now that he was getting to know his uncle he realised he had the greatest respect for Roseanne, and Simon Kershaw was not a man who would be easily duped. More than that, Roseanne was not the type of woman who would resort to cheating, or who would ever need to cheat. He had been frustrated and tired and he had been a complete fool to blurt out such stupid accusations.

For the first time in his life he had met a woman whose character and mind matched his own. She stimulated him both mentally and physically. He missed her terribly when they were apart. That had never happened to him before. But maybe he and Roseanne hadn't grown as close as he'd thought . . .

*　*　*

Roseanne was used to Euan emailing her every day, sometimes two or three times a day, if he considered her reply allowed a discussion. But this was Thursday and she had heard nothing from him since Monday. He would be leaving hospital and going to stay at Ashburn today, but there was no last message to confirm this, as she'd expected. Maybe he felt so happy to be getting out of hospital that he no longer needed contact with her. She ought to be pleased for him, but she felt bereft and down in spirits. The truth was, she missed their lively conversations. Even the emails they exchanged held hidden messages, teasing, flirting, provoking — bringing him closer in mind, if not in body. Even when they disagreed on a subject they enjoyed a stimulating debate. She had still not heard from Euan when Mr K came into her office late on Thursday afternoon.

'You will be going down to Ashburn this weekend, won't you, Roseanne?' he asked.

'I don't know.' She looked up at him. 'How is Euan? Is he home from the hospital?'

'Yes, I telephoned at midday. He's fine. Haven't you heard from him?'

'No, not a thing. I suppose he has plenty to occupy his time now without contacting me.'

'Well I'm sure he'll be pleased to be home, but he was asking plenty of questions about you on Monday evening when we visited him at the hospital.'

'Monday? I haven't heard from him since then. What did he want to know?'

'He was asking about the tricks you and young Binny used to play when you were younger. He wanted to know your sister's proper name. When are you going to introduce the two of them? He'll get a surprise when he sees how alike you are, at least in looks.'

'Ye-es. I suppose he will,' Roseanne answered, frowning thoughtfully.

'Anyway, I was hoping you'll be coming down to Ashburn, because I want to go to a sale of Aberdeen Angus cattle on Friday down in the Lake District and I thought Aileen might like to go with me and see a different part of the country. She'll not leave Euan alone in the house, though, in case he has a fall while his leg is still in plaster. I'm going down to Ashburn this evening. I need to leave early tomorrow morning. Can you arrange to get down to Ashburn by lunchtime tomorrow?'

'Yes, I suppose I could if you're sure

that's what Euan and your sister would like me to do.'

'Of course I'm sure. I imagine they'll be delighted. Aileen wants to see the Lake District but she would worry in case Euan does anything silly when there's nobody there. He's pretty good on his crutches but he's insisting on hauling himself upstairs to go to bed. I told him I'd ask Jock to help me get a bed down to the sitting room ready for him coming home but he wouldnae hear of it.'

'Something must be keeping him busy when he's never been in contact. I suppose he'll be picking up the threads of his business with his staff. He emailed me every day when he was in hospital.' Roseanne didn't realise how despondent she sounded and Simon Kershaw looked at her shrewdly. Aileen insisted young Euan was more interested in Roseanne than she had ever known him be with any other girl. A match between them would please him greatly, so long as his nephew didn't want to take Roseanne off to Australia or America. He had meant it when he told Euan he couldn't manage without her. He pulled at his lower lip and eyed her thoughtfully.

'We expected Euan would be in high spirits now he's home, but Aileen says he seems a bit out of sorts. I reckon he'll be missing all the pretty nurses running after him,' he said with a chuckle. 'He's been in touch with his colleagues. He says business is going well so that can't be troubling him. Aileen told me on the phone she'd never known him so grumpy and short-tempered, but as I reminded her, he's never been incapacitated before and it was a nasty break he had to his leg. I expect he's missing the globetrotting. Better him than me. I'm glad to be home. Maybe you'll be able to cheer him up a bit.'

'I'll do my best,' Roseanne said, 'but Rob hasn't been the brightest spirit around this week either, and I haven't managed to cheer her up.'

'Aye, well, it's time the lassie settled down in one place and got a proper job.'

Roseanne laughed. Uncle K had never considered modelling clothes a proper job and Roseanne suspected he would be shocked if he knew how much she earned while she was at the top of her career. Her thoughts returned to Euan. She wondered why he hadn't replied to her last email. Would he welcome her at Ashburn as much as his uncle expected? Every instinct told her there was something not quite right. She went back over their last meeting, but she couldn't think what she had said or done to upset him.

12

Euan was alone at Ashburn when Roseanne arrived. She greeted him with her usual light kiss and asked how he was doing, but he caught her hand and pulled her closer, looking at her neat, well-kept nails as he did so.

'Don't I get a better kiss than that? One like you gave me on Tuesday?' he asked, unable to resist testing her straight away. She blinked at him.

'Tuesday? I didn't see you on Tuesday. I haven't seen you since Sunday evening. Perhaps you've been flirting with that pretty nurse — Pamela isn't it?'

'Nope. I didn't flirt with any of the nurses.' He eyed her quizzically. 'Would you be a teeny bit jealous if I had?'

'Of course not,' she answered too quickly. 'How could I be? I've no claims on you.' She knew her voice sounded brittle, but she was still wondering why he had been too busy to send her any emails. If she was honest, she would admit to being jealous, but only to herself, and that was bad enough. His attitude seemed odd. Why was he watching her so closely? She tried to pull her hand away but he gave a tug, pulling her onto his knee.

'Your leg!' she gasped.

'There's nothing wrong with this leg. And we're all alone for the weekend, remember? Now give me a Tuesday kiss.'

'A Tue — '

He silenced her by fastening his mouth firmly on hers and giving her a very thorough kiss, awakening a desire she was struggling to control so that she was flushed and confused by the time he released her.

'That's what I mean — except this is even better than the one you gave me.'

'I-I don't know what's come over you,' she stammered. 'Euan, you're muddled. Are you still on medication? I never saw you on Tuesday and it was not me who kissed you like that anyway, not while you were in the hospital. You know by now I don't do that sort of thing in public places. Anyway, I've been at work all week. I left here very early Monday morning. Did you think I was somewhere else?' she asked with a frown. 'Is that why you didn't email me all week?' Euan was watching her closely and he thought he detected a little hurt in her green eyes.

'Did you miss my emails?' he asked softly.

'Yes. No. Who else have you been kissing?' She tried to pull away and stand up but he held her firmly.

'You are the only girl I have kissed since I arrived in Scotland. You, or your double,' he added, his eyes fixed on her face.

'My double?' She laughed incredulously. Then her smile died. 'My double, did you say?' she repeated sharply. He could almost see her mind working. Her green eyes widened as she stared back at him. 'You're not muddled, are you? You *do* think you saw me on Tuesday. B-but I don't understand.'

Euan believed her. His spirits rose. She hadn't been trying to deceive him or play any tricks to get rid of him then. But her sister had, and he wanted to know why.

'What don't you understand, Rose-anne? Why I should be kissing your double — or rather why should she be kissing me? Not that I minded the way she kisses,' he teased, exaggerating wickedly.

'Are you telling me my sister Robinia came to visit you in hospital while I was at work?'

'You tell me. Somebody came, and if it wasn't you it was your double.'

'Rob is my younger sister. We are quite alike when we wear the same sort of clothes, but not when she's dressed and made up for modelling. But why should she come all this way to see you, and why didn't she tell me she was coming? Did she pretend to be me?'

'Yes. No. Well, if I'm honest I jumped to conclusions as soon as she walked in the door, but she didn't contradict me. She looks incredibly like you but I soon began to suspect. Your kisses were much more chaste at the hospital, though I know you can do better . . . ' His eyes were dancing and her colour deepened. 'Did you know you have promised to go with me to London to meet two of my colleagues?'

'London? You never mentioned that to me.'

'I mentioned it on Tuesday and you promised to advise me.'

'I did?' Roseanne frowned. 'Let me go, Euan.' Her soft mouth had tightened. 'I need to telephone Rob. She's been on edge all week. I thought it was because her friend Jonathan has gone to London. I know this relationship is serious for her because she's promised to introduce him to me and Mother, and she had him staying at the flat while I was away. We never keep secrets from each other — not usually.'

'I'll let you go on condition you bring the phone here. I need reassurance.'

'You need reassurance? Euan Kennedy, I never met any man who needed less reassurance!'

'It's true. I need to know you haven't been playing tricks to get rid of me — like you did with Lord Gallaby's manager.'

Roseanne stared at him, her cheeks colouring. 'Who told you about that?'

'Jock McIntyre mentioned it, and Uncle Simon said it was because you considered him a nuisance. I wondered if you considered me a nuisance too, and that's why you sent your sister.'

'I admit it was not very nice of us, and Rob did go a bit too far, but we were inexperienced teenagers then and she could always deal with unwanted suitors better than I could. I'm a big girl now. You'd be in no doubt if I thought you were a nuisance.'

'So prove I'm making a bit of headway then, and give me another kiss to reassure me before you telephone.'

Roseanne bent closer, intending to give him her usual kiss on his cheek, but he turned his head and held her as he gently teased her lips with the tip of his tongue. Roseanne slid off his knee and knelt in front of him. She might be chaste in public but when she was aroused she had all the fiery passion of her sister, and more. She could feel Euan's own reaction hard against her and she pressed even closer until he drew back with a low groan of desire.

'Dear God, Roseanne, have you any idea what you do to me? I want you. I need you. I must have you even if I have to wait for the rest of my life.'

Roseanne looked into his face. The laughter had gone now and he looked both vulnerable and determined.

'I've never met a woman I wanted for more than a week,' he murmured, 'but I know I want you for life. I promise to give you time to learn to love me as I love you. Will you give me a little hope, Roseanne? Will you let me buy you an engagement ring?'

Roseanne's spirits soared, but she had to be sure. 'Euan, you only think like that now because you've been ill. I'm the only young woman you've seen recently, except for the nurses. If I'm not mistaken, there were at least two of them who would have liked to meet you when they were off duty.'

'Maybe they would, but I was too busy longing for Fridays, and your visits, to notice anyone else. I've been through hell this week wondering if you had sent your sister down to get rid of me.'

'Is that why you didn't get in touch or email me? Were you sulking?'

'Sulking? God no, that's not my style. But then, I didn't think sitting there fretting over a woman was my style either. It seems I was wrong. I was afraid to email you in case you really did want to be rid of me now I'm nearly recovered and you don't need to feel guilty anymore.'

'Of course I don't want rid of you.

I'll bring that phone across and see what my sister has been playing at, but you'll have to release me first.'

'Give me one more kiss and then I'll let you go as far as the telephone.'

It was quite a while later before Roseanne brought the phone as near to him as the cord would allow. She pressed the speaker phone. Rob answered straight away and the disappointment in her tone was obvious.

'Oh it's you, Ros. Did you have a good journey?' she asked flatly.

'I did. Sorry to disappoint you, Rob. I take it Jonathan's not back yet?'

'No. I thought it would be him phoning to say the trains are running late or he's missed a connection.'

'Well don't forget I want to inspect him before you do anything hasty — like getting married. Now I have a question for you, dear little sister, and I want the truth. Were you down here visiting Euan?'

'Aah.' Rob drew in her breath. 'So he did guess. I should have told you about that.' She sighed heavily. 'I wanted to do some inspecting of my own before you marry Euan.'

Roseanne gasped; her eyes widened and colour flamed in her cheeks. She glanced at Euan. He was watching her intently as he listened. 'I never gave you the impression that I . . . That we . . . That I was considering getting married to anyone,' she said indignantly.

'I know you didn't, Ros, but I can tell he's got under your skin and I've never known any man who could do that before. You have never been affected the way you are now. You're so protective where he's concerned. I guessed you didn't want me to see him, or play any of our old games.' Roseanne's colour deepened and she wished she'd never put the speaker phone on for Euan to listen in, but the damage was done and he was grinning widely. She looked away from him as Robinia went on. 'I've been feeling bad about visiting him without your permission. I didn't mean to impersonate you, but when I entered his room he thought I was you, and his eyes lit up like stars so I went along with the pretence, thinking he would say something when he realised. But he didn't, and I was not very well primed for swapping places so I couldn't stay long. My visit didn't do much good. How did he know I was not you?'

'He knew I was supposed to be at work. Anyway, he said your kisses were different.' She arched an eyebrow in Euan's direction and pulled a face. He grinned at her.

'Oh, did he? That's because he's not the man I'm going to marry.'

'So why did you do it, Binny?'

'Don't call me that, Ros, even if you are mad at me. I am sorry, honestly. It was a wasted journey and I've been feeling bad about it all week. I'm glad you know about it now, but I don't want you to get hurt, Ros.'

'Hurt? Why should I get hurt?' Ros frowned at the phone. There was a pause, then Robinia went on in a rush, and Roseanne knew she was nervous.

'Well for one thing, his job takes him all over the world and his base is in America, isn't it?'

'Y-yes,' Roseanne said, and all her own doubts came flooding back. She had wondered whether Euan would fly away as soon as he was well enough and leave her heart broken. Even if he did think he loved her and wanted to marry, did she want to leave everything and everyone she loved to move to the other side of the world? Could she leave Uncle K in the lurch?

Euan saw the doubts chasing each other across her expressive face and he tugged urgently at her hand. 'I'll never leave you,' he whispered. 'She's wrong . . .'

'Is Euan there?'

'Yes. He says he'll never leave me, but — '

'Well something else has troubled me, Ros.' She lowered her voice, unaware that the speaker phone was on at Roseanne's end. 'Even if he did ask you to go with him to America . . .'

Again Euan tugged her hand, but this time she was listening to Rob. 'He — he was talking about having to sell part of his company. Has he told you that?'

'No.' She glanced at Euan. 'But he has mentioned going to London.'

'If he's short of money . . . well, you should make sure he's not after your share in Uncle K's company.' Roseanne gasped, but Rob went on quickly. 'After all, you own almost half of Kershaw & Co. and it has grown rapidly since you took over the business side. Even if your capital is all tied up, your share is bound to be worth a lot now. Uncle K told Mother you were his greatest asset. Grandpa wouldn't have wanted you to lose your inheritance to a man who — '

'You've said enough, Robinia!' Roseanne snapped. Her face was pale now. She saw Euan scowling. 'You can't think much of my judgment if — '

'Oh I do, I do, Ros. Please don't be mad at me. I trust your opinions implicitly on everything — except men. You've never shown serious interest in anyone before. Some men can be proper bastards.'

'Don't you think I know that?' Roseanne's tone was cold. 'Is that your opinion of Euan?'

'To tell the truth I came away more confused than ever. He seemed a nice guy as far as I could tell, but he didn't give much away.' She strove to lighten the conversation. 'If I hadn't already fallen in love with Jonathan I think I would have found your Euan a challenge.'

'You'd better stick to your own man, little sister. Have a good weekend with him. I'll see you on Monday — but no more interfering in my life. Do you understand, Robinia?'

'Okay, okay. I'm sorry, Ros, truly I — ' But Roseanne had already cut her off.

'I'm sorry about that,' Roseanne said, still frowning with annoyance as she put the phone back in place. 'I shouldn't have put it on the speaker phone.'

'Which bit are you sorry about,

Roseanne?' Euan asked, unsmiling, his grey eyes bleak now.

'Rob coming to inspect you of course. I knew she was feeling uneasy about something.'

'I don't care about that. She was watching out for you. Maybe I'd do the same if I had a sister.'

'She was interfering. I can make up my own mind about who I want for my friends,' Roseanne said.

'I'm sure you can,' he said coolly. 'So when were you going to tell me you are a partner in Kershaw & Co.? Why did you let me make such a fool of myself over the journal entries?'

'Oh, that,' Roseanne said, brushing it aside. 'That's not important.'

Euan blinked. She owned a share in the company, as well as half the farm, and that was not important. There was no end to the surprises she presented.

'Not important? Of course it's important. You let me make a bloody fool of myself. Then you go all cold and angry on me for misjudging you. Why didn't you tell me? Did you think like your sister — that I might be interested in your fortune?'

Roseanne sighed and closed her eyes despairingly for a moment. 'Mr K will tell you more about the business when he knows you better.'

'*You* should have told me. Why didn't you explain instead of getting so angry with me?'

'It is not my place to explain. It is your uncle's business. Anyway, I was hurt that you didn't trust me. I am proud of being honest and trustworthy, but you misjudged me so badly.'

'You must admit I had reason to wonder about the figures, and I only had my uncle's interests at heart. Now I know him better, I realise he doesn't need me to watch out for him. I'm sorry, truly sorry, Roseanne. I should have followed my instincts. They all told me you were different and as trustworthy as my own mother. It's just that the figures seemed to tell a different story. Surely you can see that?'

'Yes, I understand why you jumped to conclusions, but you almost accused me of fraud.'

'Oh, surely not.'

'That's what it would have been if I'd been taking money dishonestly.'

'Oh God.' Euan rubbed his temple. 'I made a terrible mistake by suspecting you at all, even with the figures in front of me. Can you forgive me?'

'I think we understand each other better now.'

Euan noticed she had not said she did forgive him, and he couldn't blame her. 'I see . . . ' A reluctant smile tugged at the corners of his mouth. He reached out a hand to her. She took it and he drew her back down beside him onto the settee.

'You're a very complex woman, Roseanne Fairfax, and I think it will take me a lifetime to discover all the facets that make up your intriguing personality. Please say that we can be engaged so that I can proclaim you are mine and begin learning all about you?'

His voice was deep and gruff with emotion. His arms tightened, holding her closer.

Roseanne was silent, chewing her lower lip. She loved Euan, but did she love him enough to give up everything she held dear and move with him to the other side of the world? Especially knowing he would often be away from home, travelling to do his work, leaving her alone. Then what about Uncle K? He had grown to depend on her. How soon would they be able to train someone to take her place? Her heart sank at the thought of leaving the work she loved, and Uncle K had been like a father to her — a father and a friend. And the flat! What about the flat she had so recently bought with Robinia? How could she tell her sister she wanted to sell her share in it? It was doubtful if they would get their money back if they sold again so soon, not to mention the legal fees.

'Must I take your silence as a sign you think you will never be able to love me, as I love you?' Euan asked quietly, loosening his hold on her and struggling to sit up so that he could look into her face.

'Oh Euan, there will be lots of things we still have to discover, and things we shall disagree about, but I wouldn't want to marry a man who didn't have a mind of his own. I love you already, but . . . but . . .'

'But not enough to marry me? I promise to be patient, to wait as long as you need, my darling girl. Will you allow me to buy you an engagement ring so that I can tell the world I mean to win you?'

'It isn't that I don't love you enough, Euan. The trouble is, I love my family too, and my job. I shall be letting Rob down over the flat if I go with you to America, and I shall be forsaking your uncle. And — and I can't ask him to pay out my share of the company, however short of money you are for your own business. It would cripple Kershaw & Co., and he would have to sell, and I would feel responsible for all the people who would lose their jobs.' Her eyes filled with unexpected tears.

'Hey, hey, hold on, Roseanne. Who ever said anything about you giving up your job or deserting your sister or taking you to live in America? Don't you see, my darling? I am selling a quarter share of my company to each of two younger colleagues on condition that they will do most of the travelling for the next five to ten years. I want to put down roots in Scotland with you. I had a lot of time to think while I was in hospital and I know now that wherever you are, that's where I want to be. We can easily afford to leave the money in the flat and let your sister live in it, for as long as she wants.'

'You really mean you would give up your own business for me?' Rosanne turned to him, her green eyes shining, but then she shook her head slowly. 'I couldn't let you do that, Euan. You built it up from nothing. You would grow to resent it, and — '

'Listen, Roseanne.' He took her gently by the shoulders. 'I am only selling half my business, and I shall still have the major share and control. That's why we must go to London to iron out the details. Each of my two colleagues will buy a quarter of my company, or maybe twenty per cent each, depending on how committed they can afford to be. Sometimes I may have to make journeys to other countries, but most of the time I expect to be able to deal with everything from here.'

'You really think it could work for you? You think we could stay together in Scotland?'

'Not only in Scotland, but right here at Ashburn if Uncle Simon will agree to sell us his share of this house. I remember you said if you had to choose this is where you would like to be. Well, I can fix up a system so that most of your work can be done from here too. We can travel up to the factory for a few days each month if necessary. Perhaps we could use the empty flat next to Uncle Simon's. I have a feeling he will agree to almost anything rather than part with his perfect P.A.' He grinned at her.

'I can't believe you would turn your life upside down for me,' Roseanne breathed.

'Dare I hope that is a yes, you will marry me then?' Euan asked, with laughter in his voice. 'It isn't the enthusiastic reply I'd hoped to get when I asked a girl to marry me.'

'You mean you've never asked anyone before?' Roseanne looked him steadily in the eye.

'No. I've never met anyone I wanted to marry until I met you, my darling.'

'Well that's all right then.' Roseanne's green eyes sparkled before she threw her arms around his neck and kissed him with all the passion he had longed for.

'Ah, my Roseanne. I love you more with every second, and I don't want to waste any time in making you mine.'

'I think Mother will succeed in persuading Rob to have a grand affair for her wedding — one last fling in her world of models and photographs — but I would like to have a quiet wedding. Would you mind if we got married here, in the village church? I could ask Uncle K to give me away.'

'Quiet, did you say?' Euan gave a spurt of laughter. 'I guarantee everyone in the village will be there, and they'll love it.' His voice deepened. 'And so shall I, my darling Roseanne.' It was a long time before either of them got around to discussing wedding plans.

We do hope that you have enjoyed reading this large print book.

Did you know that all of our titles are available for purchase?

We publish a wide range of high quality large print books including:
Romances, Mysteries, Classics
General Fiction
Non Fiction and Westerns

Special interest titles available in large print are:
The Little Oxford Dictionary
Music Book, Song Book
Hymn Book, Service Book

Also available from us courtesy of Oxford University Press:
Young Readers' Dictionary
(large print edition)
Young Readers' Thesaurus
(large print edition)

For further information or a free brochure, please contact us at:
Ulverscroft Large Print Books Ltd.,
The Green, Bradgate Road, Anstey,
Leicester, LE7 7FU, England.
Tel: (00 44) 0116 236 4325
Fax: (00 44) 0116 234 0205